Not Ever

-a Novel by Amanda Sue King-

Chapter 1

The first day of spring. No clouds dared mar the ocean-blue sky. Not today. The fragrance of lilacs saturated the soft breeze with their intense sweet aroma as robins hopped along—"busy with life," Mama would say—keeping their ear to the ground. Listening. Waiting.

I stood under a lonely pine tree and watched from a distance as men tore the façade of artificial grass from the rectangular patch of soil. Then they removed the purple covers from the chairs where the family had recently sat. Stands and sprays of flowers had already been carelessly tossed aside, the personal touch they'd tried so hard to show now so factitious. The purr of a motor penetrated the air as Mama's coffin disappeared into the grave.

I covered my mouth, muffling the uncontrollable sobs, and sank to my knees. *Why, God? She deserved better. I deserved—*

"Stop it, Mamie." No longer would I pray to a God who didn't exist. For four years I'd begged and pleaded for Him to let my mother live. Heal her of the cancer ravaging her body, for my father to love and respect her just once…to give her a reason to live.

The roar of a different type of motor drew my attention back to the gravesite. The thud of dirt hitting Mama's casket became deafening. I pushed myself up, covered my ears with my hands, and ran from the cemetery, snagging my dress on the iron gate.

Hot tears rolled down my face and dripped from my chin as I drove through the streets of Clarksdale. Emotions raged inside, all muddled together—anger, sadness, exhaustion, loss, and *disgust*. By now, our house would be full of family—most I'd never seen before today—and friends, all stuffing their faces with food. How could anyone think of eating at a time like this? But Mississippians prided themselves on Southern idealism. There'd be enough fried chicken and casseroles to satisfy the heartiest appetite.

I'd never find contentment there. Not in that house. I'd watched my mother give all she had, and for what? She died of something much worse than cancer. No man would ever drain the life from me. Not now. Not ever.

I turned left onto Highway 61 and headed north.

"It's two o'clock; do you know where your children are?" The radio announcer laughed. Two in the morning. I'd been gone for over nine hours. Surely, Dad had found the note. He couldn't have missed it. With a rubber band, I attached it to the whiskey bottle he had stashed under his truck seat. My remarks short and to the point. *I know about your new woman. So did Mama. She couldn't take it anymore. Neither can I. I won't be back.*

I rolled down the driver's window. Cool air whipped strands of hair in every direction, occasionally slapping me in the face with a sting, reminding me to stay awake. The winding road demanded undivided attention. I'd taken pig trails and two-lane highways looking for nothing in particular, yet wondering if I'd know it when I saw it—a safe place, a new home. One free of painful memories.

My headlights flash across a sign—Ferry Ahead. I backed off the gas pedal, sat up straighter, and leaned forward. "Where is it?" I pulled closer to the water's edge but saw no ferry or bridge. Then, with eyes burning with fatigue, I spotted a light in the distance moving oh-so-slowly.

The rumble of an approaching vehicle disrupted the quiet solitude. For the first time since I left Clarksdale, fear wormed its way in. Shivers rippled down my spine. What was I doing out in the middle of nowhere? Just me and whoever!

I rolled up the windows and locked both doors of the MG, glad the chilly night air had prevented me from driving with the top down.

What appeared to be a truck topped the hill. Headlights reflecting in the side and rearview mirrors temporarily blinded me. Minutes later, it stopped several yards behind. A door slammed. The silhouette of a man—tall, broad shouldered, wearing a cowboy hat—staggered toward me. I slammed the car into reverse, spun the wheel, and punched the gas pedal.

"Hey! Are you crazy?" A man stood scant inches away. "Wait a minute."

No way. Shifting into first, I swerved around him and drove much too fast, constantly checking the mirrors to see if he followed. Tears blurred my vision. Breathe. I needed to breathe. What did he want? My fingers ached from gripping the steering wheel too tight. I tried to find a sense of calm, knowing a truck wouldn't be able to outrun a MG Midget on these curvy Arkansas roads.

After I spent forty-five minutes racing down the highway with no signs of being followed, the lack of sleep tugged at my eyelids. That's when I noticed Hattie's Restaurant with the Closed sign secured in the front window. I pulled around to the far corner and parked in what I hoped would be the safety of darkness and propped my head against the seat. Just a quick twenty minutes…thirty at the most.

— ⁕ —

"Wake up, sleepyhead," Mama's voice called out as she tapped on my bedroom door. She tapped again.

"Are you okay in there?" Only this time the voice wasn't Mama's.

My eyelids flew open. I jumped, banging my right knee against the steering column, and jerked away from the unfamiliar face staring through the side window. "What do you want?"

"Just making sure you're all right before I open up." The plump, middle-aged brunette nodded toward the restaurant. "It's four thirty. We don't officially start serving for another hour, but it won't take but a few minutes to get a pot of coffee ready, if you're interested. Might make you feel better."

Coffee did sound good. I scanned the parking lot, unlocked the door, and then grabbed my purse and Atlas before stepping out of the car. "You run this place by yourself?"

"Nah. The others'll be along in a bit." She fumbled with a set of keys and headed for the door. "I just manage the joint. Here." She took a flashlight out of her purse and shoved it in my hand. "Hold this while I get us in and turn some lights on. What year's your car?"

"Seventy-two." I followed her inside. "Bought it used four years ago, right after I graduated from high school. My mother helped me pick it out. Red is…*was* her favorite color."

"Not bad looking for eight years old. Sit anywhere you want." She motioned toward tables and booths on either side of the room. "I'll brew us up something guaranteed to get our hearts pumping. The name's Doris by the way."

"Yeah, well, I'm surprised my heart's still working after you scared the liver out of me."

She laughed and disappeared into what had to be the kitchen while I located the restroom. What a disheveled mess. Torn dress, tangled hair, streaked makeup. A wet paper towel and hairbrush helped, but what I needed was to land somewhere.

Back in the dining area, I slid into one of the front booths and began studying the Arkansas and Missouri maps, trying to figure where to head next. Doris set two white mugs of steaming tar-black liquid and a small pitcher of cream on the table. "Where you headed, sugar?"

"I don't really know, yet."

She flopped down across from me and cocked her head. "What do you mean? You in some kinda trouble?"

"No!" I answered much too quickly.

Her eyebrows rose. Who could blame her? I looked a sight, *and* she'd just found me sleeping in my car. "Runnin' from a bad marriage?"

"You might say that." It wasn't a total lie.

"Mountain Home," she blurted out.

"What?"

"Mountain Home. It's about an hour's drive west of here. You stay on this road," she pointed toward the highway out front, "until you get to a ferry—"

I didn't dare tell her I'd already been there but left when some massive dude weaved his way mere feet from where I sat.

"You like to fish?" she asked.

I stared at her, wondering how much of the one-way conversation I'd missed.

"Fish. You know, like with a rod and reel? Mountain Home's known for its fishing and beautiful lakes. It's a hotspot during the summer months, lots of tourists, but during the off-season…oh, it's the most peaceful place on earth. A regular paradise."

Peaceful? What a concept.

"Our family used to go there every October and rent a cabin near Bull Shoals Lake for the weekend." Doris traced the rim of her mug with her finger. "I'd move in a minute if my husband wasn't tied in tight with his family's business…one of only two grocery stores in town."

I turned the Atlas toward her. "Show me."

"Hmm, let me see. Here you go." She took her pen and circled a spot then angled the map for me to see. "Say, you hungry? I can fix us some toast."

"No thanks. Coffee's plenty." Although I hadn't eaten in two or three days, my stomach still felt like it'd reject anything not liquid.

"Sure?"

"I'm sure." I reached for my purse. "How much do I owe you?"

She held her hand up and smiled. "It's on the house."

"I can't—"

"Forget it. I won't take your money…. You never told me your name."

"Mamie. Mamie Carlson." I stood, downed the last of the now-lukewarm liquid, and headed toward the door.

"Hope you find what you're looking for, Mamie."

"Thanks." I didn't tell her, but all hope died three days ago with my mother's last breath.

"Wait." She propped her left hip against the green vinyl bench. "Call me nosy, but I'm curious, which way you headed?"

"I'm still thinking."

Doris slipped her hand inside her pocket and pulled out a quarter. "How about heads you go left, tails you go right." She flipped the coin high in the air, caught it, and slapped it down on the table.

"Left being Mountain Home, right being anywhere?"

"That's correct." A smile teased the corners of her mouth. "So what will it be, Mamie Carlson?"

With one hand on the doorknob and the other one on my hip, I locked eyes with her. "I'll play your game. What does it say?"

"Come see for yourself."

Chapter 2

Patches of pink and purple, marbled with orange, smeared the hazy-blue sunrise as the ferry chugged across Norfork Lake. Diesel fumes from the small tug polluted the air and stung my nose when I stepped outside of my car. Laughter and small talk echoed off the clear bluish water, so different from the muddy brown back home. I couldn't help but wonder if this laid-back pace was a reflection of what lay ahead in Doris's hamlet.

"Look, Daddy, a fish," a child squealed. "What kind is it?"

"Didn't see it, son." The man placed an arm around the boy's shoulder. "Was it a big one?"

The boy held up his two small index fingers, carefully eyeing each as he spread them a good two feet apart. "This long."

The young, sandy-haired deckhand laughed. "That's one whale of a fish. 'Course, we've got some big ones in here. Could've been a bass or crappie." He smacked his lips. "Trout's my favorite. Cook you up a mess with some fried potatoes. Ooo-eee."

I moved next to the woman dressed in a white nurse's outfit. "Excuse me. Once we make it to the other side, how much further to Mountain Home?"

"About six or eight miles. It's not far…just—"

"You staying or passing through?" the sandy-haired worker interrupted.

"It depends. I haven't seen the town yet."

He hopped up and took a seat on the railing I supposed was designed for our safety. However, with all the open space between the deck and the metal bar, there was little to keep a rambunctious child from going overboard. "You'll love it." He winked. "I'll gar-antee it. What kind of work you looking for?"

"*If* I stay, whatever I can find…whatever pays the most."

"You might try the hospital. They're always looking for nursing assistants," the woman offered. "I work for one of the doctors in Mountain Home, so I'm not sure of any openings right now."

"You make *this* commute every day?"

She smiled. "Monday thru Friday. It's not so bad, really. In fact, I appreciate having a chance to enjoy God's creation. No two are ever the same." She pointed toward the sky.

"Say," the worker pushed himself off the railing and landed on his feet beside me, "you ever wrapped meat?"

"I beg your pardon?"

"M&H is looking for a meat-wrapper. 'Course, old man Harry is tight as the bark…well, you get the picture. The ad in the newspaper didn't say how much the job paid, just looking for someone with experience. Then there's the Holiday Inn. They need extra help from time to time at the restaurant and in housekeeping. Baxter Lab might be another place to try. Curious," he squinted, "couldn't help but notice your Mississippi tag. What brings you to this neck of the woods?"

"Well…" What do I say?

"Hey!" he shouted and flung his arms in the air. "You boys settle down back there. Okay, that's it." He stormed off, apparently back on the job. "Everybody in your rigs. We'll be docking soon."

I thanked the nurse for her help and sauntered back to my car, grateful the ruckus prevented me from answering. I couldn't help but laugh as I remembered the look on Doris's face before she lifted her hand from the coin. Like Sylvester with the canary, she enjoyed the suspense and wasn't at all surprised to see heads laying right-side up. Maybe I should've inspected that quarter before leaving. Too late now.

The man in the tug angled the barge to the left and reversed the engine.

In Mountain Home only five days, and I already had a job. Mom would be proud of me…or would she? I stared at the amethyst ring she and Dad had given me when I turned thirteen. More of a gift from Mom than Dad, I always suspected. She never did stop trying to pretend we were a normal happy family. Whatever. I didn't want to think about him.

I slipped the black hairnet in place and glanced in the mirror. Memories of Miss Lucy, the lunchroom lady from my high school days, flashed through my mind—white apron, skinny as a stray dog, jet-black dyed hair. Of course, anyone could still see my flaming red curls peeking out through the woven mesh, but still, the overall picture screamed disaster. Maybe I'd pick up a clear shower cap next trip to Walmart. Anything would be an improvement.

"Hurry up in there," Harry—Mr. Aldridge—ordered. "It's almost eight."

I twisted my watch around: ten till. My hours were from eight to five, six days a week, and I'd only been hired because I lied about having experience, and he hadn't asked for references. How did I let Doris talk me into this?

"You can do it," she'd said when I stopped in after exhausting all my options—and almost half of what little I had left after Mama's funeral expenses. Quick as a wink, she bundled me off to her in-laws' grocery. For the next hours, her husband had me wrap, unwrap, and rewrap every head of cabbage in the produce bin. I had an idea of what to do. But Mr. Aldridge was no idiot, and he expected me to keep up with two butchers *and* manage the deli counter. My hand shook as I reached for the bathroom doorknob.

"It's about time." His growl roared into laughter as he patted me on the shoulder. "Don't look so worried. You'll do fine. I've got a feeling about you."

I stood up straight and peered into his steely-blue eyes. "What's that supposed to mean?"

"That!" The old man pointed a knobby finger in my face. "The way you look a person straight in their eyes. It says a lot. You're honest, and I'd bet my last dollar, a hard worker."

The lump of guilt wouldn't go away no matter how hard I swallowed. I couldn't do this. He'd find out sooner or later. "Mr. Aldridge—"

He held up his hand. The jingle of the tiny bell above the front door had ended our conversation. "Good morning, Mrs. McCarty. How are you this morning?" He trotted off in a rush to greet his first customer of the day.

I walked slowly to the back room where the two men were busy at work. The heavyset older one sliced off chunks of beef from the carcass with swift short strokes—barely missing his fingers—while the much younger one pushed the hunks of meat through a grinder. I'd been introduced to Dave and Jim the day Mr. Aldridge hired me but couldn't remember what name went with who. I fingered the apron strings dangling in front where I'd wrapped them back around and tied them snug.

"You goin' stand there all day or get to work?" the older butcher asked without looking up. "Grab one of those tubs of ground beef Jim has sitting off to the side and start wrapping. One pounders first.

I'll let you know when to start the two pounders."

His gruff rudeness reminded me of my father. I stood planted in place as a defiant attitude bristled through me. His you-woman-I-man approach wasn't going to cut it. To tell him off and walk away would only give him satisfaction. "Thanks…Davy, right?" The words dripped with sarcasm.

"The name's Dave," he snapped.

"Well, Dave, how about you let me know how many one-pound packages we need. Then I should be able to figure it out myself. No need in you having to keep such a close watch. Wouldn't want you to cut yourself."

Dave's hands stopped. His eyes locked on mine. His scowl reminded me of one of those short, husky bulldogs with an under bite. "Thirty…and once we finish stocking our meat cases, we've got commercial orders for patties. I *will* show you how we package them. Our clientele expect nothing but the best. When that's finished, we'll switch to bulk orders, twenty-five-pound bags. Got it?"

I forced a smile and held his gaze. "Got it."

"Good." He snorted. "That's good."

For several uncomfortable seconds, we glared at one another like two English bulldogs, sizing each other up, waiting to see who made the next move.

"Why don't I show you where we keep all our supplies?" Jim broke the silence.

Grateful for an excuse to walk away, I followed him to a side room. "What's his problem?"

Jim eased the door closed. "Dave is one of those rough, old souls that take some getting used to. He's really an okay guy."

"Right, and I'm Princess Leia."

Jim gave me a quick head to toe once over and laughed. "Yeah…well, we're glad to have you on board."

My earlier tension washed away. At least, I'd be working next to one person with a sense of humor. I'd even begun to think I could do this job, but that spark of confidence frizzled to fleeting vapor. I worked at a frantic pace all morning. Even worked through lunch, trying to catch up. But the bell, signaling another customer out front, wouldn't give me a break. Everyone was very nice but demanding. I never knew so many people to be so persnickety about sandwich meat.

"Thinner, honey. I want to be able to read the newspaper through it."

"Thick enough to put between a biscuit and know it's there."

"Could you double wrap the bologna for me? Love to eat it, can't stand the way it stinks up my refrigerator."

"Make sure it's sandwich thick."

What did *sandwich thick* mean, anyway? Thick as a slice of bread?

I didn't mind, not really. After all, they were the customers. But the one thing driving me nuts was removing the casing from the hard salami, like taking pantyhose off the fat woman in the circus—not that I'd actually ever attempted such a feat. Warm water supposedly helped loosen the clear covering, something Doris's husband showed me, but I couldn't see that it made a bit of difference.

By the end of the day, six o'clock rather than five, my back, legs, and arms ached. In spite of my exhaustion, and for the first time since my mother's death, my appetite had returned. A plate of vegetables sounded good. I tossed my grungy apron in the hopper and made a beeline for the door.

"Mamie, could I have a word with you?"

The look on Mr. Aldridge's face gave nothing away, but the fact that he turned and headed toward his office drenched me with a sickening feeling that my first day could be my last.

Chapter 3

A wave of nausea washed over me as I took the first step up the dingy, narrow stairway leading to Mr. Aldridge's office. Him saying I was honest earlier today now plagued my conscience. He'd looked into the face of a liar and been fooled, and I did nothing to correct the wrong. If only—

"Come in, Mamie. Have a seat." He pointed to the red leather chair on the other side of his desk. "Now, what did I do with your file? I had it just a second ago."

He flipped through the multiple papers scattered across his oak desk, stained dark with age. It wasn't the only antique still in use. A black rotary phone sat on the upper right corner next to a monstrosity of an adding machine with rows and rows of numbered keys on its face and a crank handle on its side. A brass desk lamp with a small chain dangling under its milky glass globe wore weeks, if not months, of dust. While a large silver-colored clock, bearing the name King Cotton hung on the wall above the four-drawer oak file cabinet. I'd bet not a single thing in this room had changed since that one-dollar bill, now framed and hanging, exchanged hands. Even the air smelled musty as if left behind from times past.

"Here it is." He pulled a binder from under the thick ledger and set it unopened in front of him. "My wife's expecting me home for supper, so I won't dally around with small talk. Let me just say, I'm a little disappointed—"

My face flamed with heat. "You don't have to say it. It was wrong of me, and you have every right to be mad. There's no excuse other than I desperately needed a job."

Mr. Aldridge furrowed his brows. "Mad? Confused at this point, but I'm certainly not angry."

I twisted my purse straps, sure my face and hair matched in color. "You're not?"

"No, of course not. I called you in here to commend you on being such a hard worker. And to say how guilty I feel starting you off at such a low salary. To offer you twenty cents more an hour, but only on one condition, no more working through lunch breaks?"

I replayed our conversation in my mind, attempting to make sense of what was happening. Was he trying to trick me? To see if I had any scruples?

He laid his arms across the desk, fingers laced together. "Do we have a deal?"

"I don't understand. You didn't call me in here to fire me?"

"To fire you? What on earth gave you that idea?"

"Oh…" I moaned and buried my face in my hands, wishing I could vaporize, float away to parts unknown, or slide through the cracks in the floor.

"What's bothering you, Mamie?"

I forced myself to look at him. "Mr. Aldridge, I've never wrapped meat." The words spewed forth, refusing to stay buried any longer. "I've never even worked in a grocery store. A guy named Wayne gave me a crash course with heads of cabbage. For three years, I worked as a teller in a bank where the only things we had to wrap were rolls of money, and even then, a machine did all the work. Nothing but a

Christmas season at a department store would come close to any type of experience for this job."

Mr. Aldridge opened his mouth, closed it, and then shifted in his chair.

"I'm sorry." I wrung my hands, wishing I could do more to right this wrong. "Maybe I should go."

"Sit," he ordered as I started to stand. His gaze cut through me like a knife. "Why? Why did you lie? Did you think I wouldn't hire you?"

"The ad said—"

"I know what the ad said. What else don't I know about you, Mamie Carlson?"

His scowl sent my heart racing in a rage of panic. "There's no reason for you to believe me." My throat constricted, making it difficult to force out. "But I've never done anything like this before, and I'll never…" Why should he believe me? "M–m–mama…would be ashamed. I'm ashamed."

"And you should be." His eyes flickered with anger.… Or was it disappointment? "Of all the problems I've had to deal with over the years—" He glanced at his watch. "A precarious situation. One I'll have to give some thought to. But for now," he scooted his chair back and stood, "my wife's expecting me."

I sat stark still, unsure what to do or say.

"If," he removed a brown felt hat from the wooden coatrack, "and I mean *if*, you want this job, be here tomorrow morning at seven thirty sharp. But I make no promises."

"Yes, sir." I pushed myself from the chair. "I'll be here."

With a nod toward the door, Mr. Aldridge dismissed me. The weight of humiliation mounted with each step. I hated myself, didn't want to see anyone, and for the first time, I wondered what it'd be like to get drunk…to drown my misery in a bottle just like I'd seen Dad do often.

I slid behind the wheel and dug through my purse for the keys. The newspaper ad—cute two-room cabin, only minutes from the lake—glared back at me. It sounded perfect last night when I spoke to the owner. "Well, won't be needing this." I wadded the clipping and tossed it on the floorboard.

So what if you promised the woman you'd meet her at seven? Without a job, you're just wasting her time.

"A lie that is half-truth is the darkest of all lies," I could hear Mom saying. She loved to read and often quoted Tennyson. And Twain, Lincoln, and of course, the Scriptures whenever she suspected me of lying as a child.

I rescued the crumpled slip of paper, searched inside my purse for the written directions, and set out for Buzzard Roost Road. What a name, but how appropriate, since by tomorrow morning, life for me in Mountain Home would, most likely, come to an end.

Buzzard Roost Road started off paved with a few potholes and soon turned into gravel. Maple, birch, and pine trees lined both sides where red squirrels scaled their bark. Birds flittered from branch to branch. But it was a dried leaf drifting across the road ahead that intrigued me most since fall had long passed. As I neared, the leaf appeared to have legs. I stopped and opened the door for a closer inspection and then quickly slammed it shut. Shivers ran down my spine. A spider, the size of my fist, strolled fearlessly across the road, oblivious to my presence. What other creatures inhabited Doris's paradise?

I shifted the car into first and continued my search for the "small, gray, wooden cabin with a blue tin roof" the woman, Mrs. French, had described. "You can't miss it," she'd said. "Three, maybe four, miles outside of town." But I'd already gone too far with no sign of the building. Time ticked away. If I didn't find an address on one of the mailboxes soon, something to push me forward, I'd be forced to backtrack. Then I saw it and an orange Mustang that didn't seem to match the blue-haired woman sitting on the top step. I pulled into the short drive and stepped out onto freshly mowed grass. Its sweet, clean smell soon surrendered to the fragrance of honeysuckle. "Mrs. French?"

"Please," she stood and smiled, "call me Fanny."

Fanny? I almost got tickled as I rolled the tall, thin woman's name over in my mind. Why would a mother brand a child with a title so hideous? But then Mamie wouldn't have been my choice, either. "Nice to meet you."

"Come." She waved me forward. "Check out the inside. It's small but darling. The perfect getaway if you asked me."

As the screen door slammed behind us, I couldn't believe my eyes. From the plush terra- cotta-colored carpet to a butcher-block countertop, the place had been completely updated. Even the almond stacked washer and dryer looked new.

"And the lake's only a few miles down the road. I'm sure you knew that, though."

"No." I turned to face her. "I haven't really done much exploring."

She shook her head. "You must take the time, dear. Life passes much too quickly to piddle it away. I came here several years ago to 'find myself' as they say. I've never regretted the move. But enough about me, what do you think of my little bungalow?"

"It's perfect—"

"Good, then I'll go over the dos and don'ts and see if we're in agreement. The rent must be paid no later than the third of each month. You'll be responsible for the electric bill. No partying, and no entertaining overnight guests…if you get my drift. And if you tear it up, you fix it. Since tomorrow's the seventh, I'll prorate the seventy-five-dollar rent, but you have to pay the fifty-dollar damage deposit up front. Any questions?"

"No...yes." If only Mr. Aldridge could give me another chance. "Would you be willing to hold it until tomorrow?"

She cocked her head to the side. "Is there a problem?"

"It's not the rules or the money." Not entirely true. "Well, it could be the money. You see, I'll know more about my financial situation in the morning. If you could give me until...say ten?"

"I really shouldn't. You know the old saying about the bird in the bush." She jingled the keys in her hand, her eyes fixed on mine as she took a moment to think. "Not a minute longer."

"Yes, ma'am."

"And you *will* call me one way or the other?"

"Yes, ma'am."

I drove away wondering what tomorrow would bring. Regardless, it was time to pack up my meager belongings and check out of the hotel...first thing in the morning.

At seven twenty, with the exception of Mr. Aldridge's car, M&H's parking lot sat empty. My fingers gripped the steering wheel, palms wet with sweat. I took a deep breath and headed for the front entrance.

"Good, you're early." He locked the door behind me and climbed the steps to his office with me in tow. "Well," he said as we both took our seats. "I had hoped you would come in today as promised rather than skip town. That shows some integrity on your part. But I'm still left with concerns. Mainly, can you be trusted? There're things more valuable than experience—trust, truth, hard work, and old-fashioned common sense. But without trust, no relationship will ever survive...not friendship, marriage, and certainly not one between employer and employee. So, we're at a crossroads. I don't know about your relationship with the Lord or even if you have one. But for me, I've learned second chances are wonderful gifts. And I'm willing to give you one, Mamie, but," he held up his right index finger as if to make a point, "you'll have to earn my trust. That's if you still want to work here. There won't be any hard feelings on my part whatever you decide."

I winced as he scooted a check with my name on it toward me.

"You choose. Any of the banks in town will cash it, and you can be on your way. Or there's work waiting for you downstairs."

Chapter 4

The bitter slice of humble pie had a sweet aftertaste. Mr. Aldridge now knew the truth, yet he still allowed me to keep the job. And with the raise he'd promised.

"I know you're busy, dear," Mrs. French said when I called. "I'll just bring the key by the market and pick up the money—one hundred and eight dollars. Fifty for the deposit and fifty-eight for the partial month's rent we discussed. Cash, dear. I only accept cash or money orders. Forgive me for not telling you sooner, but it cuts down on unnecessary headaches, you see."

"It won't be a problem," I assured her.

"And, dear, please don't get the wrong impression. Although I'm willing to go out of my way today, I'm not in the habit of chasing down my renters. Remember my list of rules."

"Yes, ma'am. I won't forget."

"Now, if I happen to be in shopping and it's close to the first of the month, then certainly you may give me the rent money…as long as you do it discreetly. There's no need in everyone knowing our business."

"I appreciate you doing this, and thanks for waiting until today for my decision."

"Certainly. You see, Harry…Mr. Aldridge, as well as his wife, and

I have been friends for years. They moved here from Wisconsin the same year I left Illinois and landed in Mountain Home. Transplanted Yankees, some would say. Anyway, if he hired you, then that's good enough for me."

I won't disappoint you, I silently promised.

"Got to run, dear. See you in a few."

Nine dollars and forty-two cents. That's all I had after the deposit to the electric company, paying Mrs. French, and purchasing a few items at one of the local mercantile during my lunch break. A flotation mattress, which someday *might* see water, for now would serve as a bed. A flat sheet, three washcloths, two towels, toilet paper, one bar of soap, plastic cups and flatware, and the smallest box of Cheer laundry detergent on the shelf. Not exactly extravagant living, still it cost more than I'd counted on.

Shortly after the last customer left, I pushed my cart up to the checkout stand, set my grocery items on the counter, and watched Mr. Aldridge ring up each one. Peanut butter and jelly sandwiches would have to do for breakfast, lunch, and supper until payday, four days away. After tax, my cash reserves had dwindled to less than five dollars. A recession the news media called it. From the looks of my pocketbook, I'd call it a full-blown depression. But I was too excited to be discouraged.

"Found you a nice place to rent, I hear." Mr. Aldridge closed the cash register drawer and handed me the receipt. "Fanny French mentioned it when she dropped by earlier."

"Moving in tonight." I held the brown paper bag close to my chest, trying not to smush the bread. "Thanks again for giving me another chance."

"Mamie, we all make mistakes when we're young…and old. But as long as you learn from it… Well, enough said."

I forced a smile and nodded, my face burning with regret and embarrassment.

"You run on." The fine lines around his eyes deepened. "Today's my anniversary, and *I'm* taking my sweetheart someplace special."

"How many years?"

He puffed his chest out. "Thirty-nine. And I'm more in love with her now than the day we got married."

I couldn't help but wonder if his enthusiasm was real. After all, most of the guys I'd ever worked with or known—especially my dad—talked about their anniversary as if it was a reminder of one of life's greatest misfortunes. But then, most of the guys I'd ever worked for would have fired me on the spot for lying.

A trickle of sweat ran down my forehead as I hauled the last few items from the car into the cabin. Without an air conditioner or fan, the nights would soon be miserable, but for now, a breeze whipped the curtains in spastic directions, spreading the heavy scent of honeysuckle throughout the small rooms.

There'd be plenty of time later tonight to put my belongings away, but I'd already decided another day wouldn't end without me exploring my new world. I laid the suitcase on the bedroom floor and opened it to retrieve a pair of cutoffs and a faded Ole Miss T-shirt. After changing, I went into the kitchen and laid two slices of bread on the counter and smeared a hefty gob of peanut butter on one of them.

"What's your name?"

I spun around with one hand clutching my chest, the other gripping the glass jar of strawberry jelly. A dirty-faced boy stood in the open doorway, barefooted and shirtless. He couldn't have been much older than four or five.

"Where did you come from?"

"Is that your car?" He pointed outside.

"Yes," I snipped and slid past him. Surely, an older child or perhaps an adult searched for the urchin. "Are you by yourself?"

"What's this?" His voice now came from inside the cabin.

Before I could respond, the child reappeared with one of his grungy fingers sticking through one of *my* bread slices.

"My supper." I glared at the discourteous intruder. "And don't look so innocent. You know what it is, and it's not yours. You want something, ask first. That includes knocking and waiting to be invited in. Understand?"

His little lip quivered. "Yeah."

"Yes, ma'am," I corrected. Who was raising this child? "Does your mother know where you are?"

"No…I mean…no, ma'am."

I stifled a giggle and eyed the fearful sprout, unsure of what to do with him. "Go ahead, you can have the bread. Would you like some jelly or peanut butter on it?"

"Uh-uh," he grunted, busy chewing away.

"Do you live around here?"

He nodded and took another bite. "You got a little boy I can play with?"

"No, I don't."

"A girl?"

"No. I'm not married."

"My mama's not married, but she gots me and my sister, Lily. She's eight."

"Really? Well…" I cleared my throat, wondering what to say to someone so young, yet way too knowledgeable. "Would you like some milk?"

"We drink Coke…Mountain Dew, Pepsi. Aaron drinks beer."

"Who's Aaron?"

"He's my mom's—"

"Brent." A man's voice bellowed from right outside.

A young girl squealed, parroting the man. "Brent."

"Are you Brent?"

The boy nodded and scanned the room, his eyes wide with an almost frantic look.

The man's voice sounded closer as he yelled, "Boy, you better answer me!"

I knelt on one knee in front of the child. "What's wrong? Who is that guy?"

"Aaron." His voice trembled. His chest heaved. "I got to go." He then whirled and ran from the cabin.

"Wait." I scrambled to my feet. By the time I made it to the door, a potbellied, scrubby-bearded man had the child by both shoulders, shaking him, his little head popping back-and-forth. A young tow-haired girl hung on one of the man's arms but was soon slung to the ground.

"You stupid brat." He growled and drew his hand back as if to slap the boy in the face.

"Hey!" I screamed and bounded from the porch.

The man looked at me but kept his hold on the frail child. "Lady, you better tend to your own business. This has nothing to do with you."

"Let go of him." I now stood less than two feet away. "I mean it. If you don't let go of him, I'll call the police." Only empty threats since there hadn't been enough time or money to have a phone installed.

"And tell them what?" He smirked. "That I'm disciplining my son?"

I quickly replayed the child's words—"he's my mom's"—in my

mind. "He's not your son. And even if he was, you have no right to hit him."

"I'm the closest thing to a father he'll ever see." He leaned down and yanked the boy to his tiptoes. "Ain't that right, boy?"

"A real father loves his children. He teaches by example, not threats and fear."

My stomach tightened as he let go of the child and moved my direction. His lip twitched then curled into a lopsided smile. "You kids get on home."

Neither of them moved.

"Now!" he roared, spit flying in my face.

The girl grabbed her brother by the hand and ran.

The smell of blue cheese and rotten onions permeated the air as the man lifted his arms and laid them across his protruding stomach. His gaze traveled down to my toes and up again as though undressing me. He cackled like a wild jackal as I stepped back.

"You're not from here, I 'spect. So let me tell you how we do things around these parts, missy. We don't threaten unless we got something to back it up with. And ain't no woman ever goin' tell a man what he can or cain't do, much less talk to a man disrespectful and get away with it. Now, I'm willing to let it slide this once," he touched my face with his finger before I could jerk away, "but if it ever happens again—"

"You'll what? Hit me? I don't think so. And if you *ever* lay a hand on Brent or the young girl, the police *will* be notified."

"Listen here!"

Before I vomited on my shoes from the smell and things got totally out of hand, I turned and stormed back to the cabin, slamming the door behind me.

"Men! You're all alike. Where does he get off hitting kids and threatening women?" The thought of the brute's hand drawn back ready to hurt the innocent child sent me into a rage all over again. "And another thing…" I flung the door open and bolted onto the porch.

Chapter 5

The beast had left. With any luck, I'd seen the last of him, but I couldn't help worrying about Brent and the girl I could only assume had to be his sister, Lily. What did their mom see in the behemoth anyway? Was she so desperate for a man, any man, that she'd settle for one so vile—one who tormented and hit her children? It wasn't as if she couldn't walk away. According to Brent, they weren't married.

My stomach boiled at the thought of being in the same house, much less the same bed, with the likes of him. I shook my head, trying to clear *that* thought from my brain as I grabbed my purse and keys.

I backed out of the driveway and took a left. In less than a mile, the number of homes increased, many of them new with natural or painted wood siding. A few single and double-wide mobile homes dotted the landscape. Long rows of mailboxes lined the left side of the road. Ahead, a sign advertising camping sites and cabins pointed off to the right. Then I spotted it—the lake Mrs. French told me about.

The sun, hanging low in the sky, cast a sparkling orange glow on ripples of water. Beautiful. Peaceful. Just like Doris had promised.

A truck, towing a boat, pulled out of the almost empty parking lot. I chose a spot close to the wooden docks and got out.

Two men fished from one of the landings, so I crossed to the other one and sat to pull off my socks and shoes. I could see clear to the sandy bottom. The water, much colder than anticipated, sent a chill rushing through me. A fish came up to investigate, almost as if smelling my feet. Perhaps it did. Its curiosity might someday land him in a hot skillet.

Maybe later, when I could afford it, I'd purchase a lawn chair and sit in this very spot and watch the sunsets.

A roar of laughter broke the spell. The two men, carrying gear and strings of fish, ambled along the wooden planks, toward the parking lot. One of them reminded me of Dad—tall, thin, tanned— and probably well on his way to being drunk, from the way he swayed and demanded attention with his raucous nonstop chatter.

A splash beneath the dock sent me scrambling to my feet as visions from the movie *Jaws* raced through my mind. "How big do these fish get around here?" I leaned over and peered between the wooden slats but saw nothing but darkness. Then movement next to the pier drew my eye.

Seconds later, a man's head popped above the surface. He removed his goggles, slid the tank from his back, and heaved it onto the dock. "Hello there." He smiled, showing brilliant white teeth contrasting his tanned face. "Sorry if I startled you."

"I wasn't…You didn't. Just admiring the view." *Stupid, stupid, what a stupid thing to say.* I cringed and waved toward the sky. "The sunset. I've got to go." I reached down and grabbed my socks and shoes.

"Wait." His brows furrowed. "Don't let me scare you off." He didn't laugh nor did I sense one hint of sarcasm. And the smug I'm-the-best-looking-thing-you've-ever-laid-your-eyes-on attitude—although he was with his dark hair, square jaw, flawless complexion, and chestnut brown eyes—didn't ooze from his every fiber.

"You're not." I cleared my throat and began again, "It's been a long day, and I have to get up early."

"You live around here or just passing through?"

I hopped around on one foot while tugging the sock on the other one. "I live here."

He wiped the amazement from his face. "Tell you what. Why don't I stay in the water while you put on your socks and shoes? I'd hate for you to take a nasty fall. Besides, it'll give me a chance to redeem myself for disturbing your afternoon. To show that the people of Mountain Home are just plain, honest, hardworking, courteous folks."

"Really?" Visions of Brent's tormenter came unbidden as I rushed to get my other sock on.

He cocked his head to the side. "Girl, you remind me of that song from a few years back, 'Somebody Done Somebody Wrong'. You don't trust anyone, do you?"

There it was, his opening line. Original. Well rehearsed. He probably thought it was smooth and perfected. Every guy had one or two. Some guys stashed away several for just such an occasion. And he wanted me to think he was somehow different.

I clenched my teeth together, refusing to allow him to see the bristled effect his words had on me, and fumbled with the right shoelace.

"Could be you haven't met the right people."

I stared into his eyes outlined by long, dark lashes, the kind most women only wished for…or purchased. "And you'd be one of those, I guess?"

No longer able to contain himself, his laughter echoed off the open water. "I think so. But don't take my word for it. Tell you what, some of us are getting together this Saturday. Right here. Four thirty.

29

What do ya say? It'd give you a chance to meet some nice people and draw your own conclusion about me?"

He was a fool if he thought… "Thanks, but no thanks."

"Oh, come on." He let go of the dock long enough to wipe his hand across his face again. "Why not take the chance?"

"Because I've got to work." I finished tying my other shoe and stood. "Besides, I'm not one to party."

"Good, then you'll fit in fine with us guys and gals. We don't do booze, drugs, or hang with those who think it's cool. We'll take out the boat. Some of us with wetsuits might ski. Great fellowship, plenty of food. What time do you get off?"

"Late!"

"Perfect." He wasn't about to give up. "Then you'll make it just in time for one of Janie's loaded-to-the-max hamburgers."

"Maybe some other time." I turned to leave.

"Hang on." Water splashing behind pulled my attention back to the lake. "I don't know your name." He tossed another black flipper next to his tanks.

The poor boy was oblivious to his predictable behavior. But every dog needs a bone now and then. "Mamie."

"As in Mamie Eisenhower?"

"That's the one," I called over my shoulder, not waiting for the wisecrack sure to follow.

"I'm Quinn."

This time curiosity bested me and had me doing an about-face. "As in?"

"Named after my father. You know, one of those family names that for some great mystery keeps getting passed down generation to generation. Well, I'm the fifth. There's been a Junior, Trip, IV, then me, and that's where the curse'll end."

No way could I douse my amusement at the disgust tinging his voice. "It must be a doozy."

"You don't want to know."

"I'd stay and try to get it out of you. But it's late and you must be miserable, not to mention waterlogged. Besides, the mosquitoes have feasted on all the blood I'm willing to give up for one evening."

"I'm not at all miserable. In fact, I've enjoyed our conversation. So will I see you Saturday, Mamie?"

"Maybe, but I wouldn't count on it," I answered before sprinting toward the faint outline of my car.

My first night in the cabin, and I keyed in on every sound, from the whippoorwills, to a cricket chirping somewhere in the front room. Another car sped past, its lights flashing through the bedroom window and across the far wall. Didn't anyone sleep around here? The clock read 1:23. I tossed the sheet back. The cricket had to go. One of us had to rest in peace before the night ended.

The next morning, I trudged into the market, still half asleep.

"It's about time." Dave looked at his watch. "Bad enough Jim's not here, but then you come dragging in ten minutes late."

My watch had six minutes till. "What happened to Jim?"

"Says he's sick, a luxury I've never had the privilege to enjoy. Well, don't just stand there—we've got orders to fill."

I tucked my purse in an empty cupboard in the back room and grabbed a clean apron off the shelf.

Dave continued with his nonstop complaints, "Busiest day of the week, and I've got to do everything. This young generation wouldn't know hard work if it—"

"What do you need me to do?"

"What you were hired to do," he shouted. "Wrap meat."

AMANDA SUE KING

"Well, since there doesn't seem to be anything ready to wrap, how about I fill in for Jim and start grinding what you've got ready?"

"And get myself fired or sued when you lose fingers or part of a hand? No, sir. A woman has no business trying to operate those kinds of machines."

"I could mutilate a finger or two with the meat slicer, but I bet you haven't lost any sleep over that, have you? Besides," I held up the wooden mallet, "it'd have to eat this up first, right?"

He hesitated, as though counting to ten, then spoke, "Okay, but let's get something straight. When I'm working, don't reach over or around me and don't touch one of these meat bins until I say so."

I nodded. "Okay."

Dave picked up a container and set it next to the grinder. "We'll work on the chili meat orders first, then hamburger. You *do* know the difference, don't you?" he slurred, his voice so condescending I wanted to slap him. "I mean, how they're ground?"

I didn't have a clue, but I knew enough to know he was trying to trip me up. "It's not my job to know. I'm just the lowly wrapper, remember? You're the butcher."

The scowl on his face deepened. "That's all right. It'd take more than a right answer, anyway, to convince me you had any experience before coming here. But for your information, chili meat's ground with a different plate—which I've already put on there—and it's ground only once."

In spite of my efforts to help, Dave's jabs were relentless. My temper would soon reach a boiling point. A reaction he'd surely take delight in, so I flipped the switch of the grinder in hopes of drowning him out and began feeding chunks of meat into the hopper.

By six thirty, my head and feet throbbed with pain as I shifted the MG and sped toward home. I looked forward to a long shower, quiet solitude, and sprawling out on my makeshift bed. It would take more

32

than a few birdcalls or the serenading crickets to keep me awake tonight. Not even the constant parade of traffic could interfere with my exhausted state. Not even—

"What in the world?" Several yards ahead, a blue-and-white truck whipped into my driveway and stopped. I slowed as a man wearing a ball cap got out and stepped onto the porch, undoubtedly lost, or was he the guy Mrs. French hired to cut the grass? Since the yard didn't need mowing and there wasn't a mower in the back of his truck, I pulled off and watched. He knocked, and then propped against one of the wooden columns, waiting. But for whom?

Chapter 6

"Can I help you?" I spoke, unable—no, not wanting—to hide the suspicious caution from my voice as I slammed the car door and stared at the unknown visitor.

The man removed his ball cap. "I'm sorry to disturb you'ins."

My mouth gaped open. The lanky man wasn't a man at all. Pimples, which had been concealed by the shadow of his hat's bill, blended with a myriad of freckles.

"My sister said I should come see you'ins."

His sister? And I thought my day couldn't get worse. The poor kid could not possibly be old enough to drive legally, and he's come…what? Courting? Soliciting for the local paper, a fundraiser for school or church? "Look, I'm sure you're a nice guy, but I'm not interested."

He stepped out of my way as I marched toward the cabin. "She don't want you to get hurt."

I skidded to a halt and eyed him. "What are you talking about?"

"Aaron. He ain't used to no woman gettin' up in his face."

It took a few seconds for my brain to process what the young man said, to understand he referred to the sorry excuse of a man I'd encountered yesterday. And his sister, no doubt, Brent's mother. "Oh, so it's perfectly okay to slap around a kid who's a fraction his

34

size, but may the world stop spinning if a woman stands in his way. What's the matter with you people?"

"It's—"

"And another thing," I stomped closer with my finger pointing toward his chest, "I didn't get in his face. He got in mine."

"Yes'm, but you don't understand."

"I sure don't. Why would your sister put up with someone so disgusting, hateful, cruel…? There aren't enough adjectives to describe the likes of him."

"Because she's scared. Besides, she ain't got no place else to go."

What's wrong with under a bridge, a tent, the local YWCA? I wanted to scream. And did in those earlier years when I tried so hard to get my mother to leave my father. But the pleas proved futile and only caused more hurt to Mama's already sad eyes.

"What about your parents? Surely, they'd rather have their daughter and grandchildren move in with them than live…" My mind searched unsuccessfully for the right words, "with him?"

"Our parents are dead. They died in an automobile accident, more'n ten years ago. Me and Tammy was raised by our Grandmaw Murt. She's tried to get Tammy to leave Aaron…. We both have. But it's no use. My sister's too scared, I'm telling you. Aaron says he'll kill her if she leaves him, and I believe he will."

"Sorry about your folks." A moment of silence passed before I trusted myself to speak again. "What about the police? Surely, they can—"

"Lady," he twisted his cap into an almost unrecognizable mess, "I'm sorry, but what part of being scared for your life don't you get? He's done put Tammy in the hospital twice…busted ribs the first time. This last'n, Aaron threw her down and kicked her so hard she lost the baby. The hospital called the police, but Tammy told 'em she fell. Don't nobody pay attention to what me and Grandmaw tell 'em. Their hands are tied, they say."

My stomach rolled. I swallowed bile, almost too afraid to ask, "What about Brent and Lily? Has he ever…?"

"He might smack 'em around—I ain't sure—but he ain't never hurt either one bad…far as we know."

"Right." How naive were these people? "It's never okay to *smack* a child, and in case you haven't thought about it, it's only a matter of time before he does worse. What about their father? Can't he get a lawyer, go to court, do something to get them out of there?"

"He drowned two months after Brent was born. My sister lost it. They'd been childhood sweethearts. Treated her like a princess, he did. She never had to work or do anything but be his wife and the kids' mama. He'd kill Aaron." His knuckles paled as he twisted the cap tighter. "I think about it sometimes." His face contorted, eyes squinted. "Killing him."

I winced and stumbled toward the porch. Those thoughts had been mine at a much younger age than him. Yet not too young to know fathers don't touch their daughters the way mine had—drunken stupor or not—and I hated him for it.

"Are you okay? I didn't mean to upset you'ins."

I looked up at the boy who nervously attempted to reshape his mangled hat. "There's got to be someone your sister can talk to who would be willing to help: an uncle, a friend…anybody?"

He stood there shaking his head.

"What about the church? Maybe they'd find her a safe place to live, help move her and the kids away from here."

"Me and Grandmaw already talked to her pastor where she used to go to church. He tried, but she wouldn't let him in. He says Tammy's got to be willing to help herself and stop living in sin."

I kicked a nearby dandelion and sent fuzzy white tendrils flying. "Man! How can he expect her to leave without help? You said yourself, she's scared out of her mind. You don't tell a starving person, 'go, be fed, be warm, and be happy' and not provide a morsel of food or something to drink. Nor does he know Tammy's not willing to get out. She doesn't know how *or* have the financial means."

"No'm, she don't have any money. She'd get a job if Aaron was to let her."

"How about Aaron? Does he work or is it his job to stay home all day and torment the neighborhood?"

"He's what some folks call a shade-tree mechanic. Helps out at a shop on the other side of town."

"Good. Then that makes things easier for us."

"Beg your pardon?"

"To set up a time when Tammy and I can talk."

Again, he shook his head. "No, ma'am, Miss…I don't know your name."

"Mamie. Plain Mamie, without the Miss, okay?"

"People call me Bud." He wiped his hand against his pant leg and held it out.

His callused hand swallowed mine with a firm shake.

"What was I about to say?" He studied the ground for brief seconds, then continued, "Tammy don't want any trouble. It's why she sent me over here. And she don't intend on Aaron finding out about it, either, much less you and her gettin' together. So if you'ins want to help, leave her and them kids alone. And if I was you, I'd keep plenty of distance from Aaron Holbrook. He's no good."

"Could you at least let her know if she ever wants to talk, or if I can help in any way, my door's open?"

"I'll tell her." He placed the cap back on his head and turned to leave.

"Bud?"

He spun around. "Yes'm?"

"Thanks...for stopping by, for not being at all like Aaron."

"You needn't worry. My Grandmaw Murt raised me better." He laughed for the first time during our conversation. "She'd wear out all the limbs on her favorite peach tree if I ever mistreated a woman."

His face lit up as he teased about the older woman who'd raised him. For a brief moment, I envied him. In spite of losing his parents, he had someone to go home to. Someone who cared.

Long after I'd pulled into the parking lot at work and turned off the car, the lyrics of the song "I Will Survive" kept playing through my head. I couldn't help but think about Tammy and my conversation yesterday with Bud.

Dave didn't look up as I walked through the back door. I wasn't at all sure *I'd* survive another day of his grumpy attitude or the grueling work with Jim out sick.

"Hey, kiddo, I hear you're after my job."

I tossed my purse inside my locker and whirled around. "Jim! You made it. How do you feel?"

"Much better. Thanks. Sorry about putting y'all in a pinch yesterday, but maybe I would've taken another day off if I'd had any idea you two could manage so well without me."

"Believe me, you were missed, and between me and you, I don't think I could've taken another day of Dave's mullygrubbing."

"He doesn't mean anything by it. Does it more out of habit than anything. Now, if he's quiet," he tilted his head and looked at me out of the corner of his eye, "there's a problem, and we *all* better watch out."

I laughed. Jim had a way about him. As though he saw only the good in people, even when the bad lay ugly-side up. "If that's the case, then he's been happy as a duck in water since the day I was hired."

"You'll get used to him."

"Never."

"Hey, you two," Dave yelled, "have I got to run this place by myself?"

Jim stepped aside and motioned for me to go first.

"Coward."

Later in the day, Mr. Aldridge found me in the break room trying to wash down the last of my sandwich.

"Here you go." He handed me an envelope with my name on it. "There's a little something extra in it, for yesterday."

"You didn't have to." I choked on the words, the peanut butter still clinging to my throat.

"Now, don't go getting all excited. It's only twenty dollars."

"But still—"

He leaned closer and whispered, "A simple *thank you* will do."

I tucked the envelope in my pocket and grinned. "Thank you."

"You're very welcome. Have you gotten settled in your new place yet?"

"Sort of."

"Had a chance to make any new friends?"

Aaron's face came to mind. But Mr. Aldridge *had* asked about friends and not enemies. Some might consider Quinn with his invitation as a potential prospect, but I didn't know him from Adam's house cat. "May I ask you something?"

"Of course." He pulled out a chair and sat across from me. "Shoot."

"If you knew a woman was being mistreated, but she wasn't willing to tell the police, what would you do?"

"Is someone mistreating you, Mamie?"

"No, sir! I don't even know the woman, never met her. It's complicated."

"Then I'd make sure I had the facts first." He peered into my eyes, his smile now gone. "Be careful. Don't ever get caught up in malicious gossip. If you're concerned, try being a friend. But I can tell you, and most policemen will tell you, when it comes to domestic disputes, it's a job best left to the professionals. Otherwise, you might end up the one hurt."

First Bud, now Mr. Aldridge. Two warnings in less than twelve hours, but I had to do something. Didn't I?

Chapter 7

Saturday evening and the parking area at the boat dock looked much different from how it appeared earlier in the week. Although not full, several trucks with empty trailers hunkered across the lot. The lake had its share of boats of all types and colors but offered no signs of anyone having a cookout.

No surprises there. Good-looking guy like Quinn couldn't possibly keep up with every girl he wooed with his sexy smile and invitation of an afternoon out on the lake.

Just as well. I didn't come with any hopes of meeting up with him anyway.

I reached for the brown paper bag on the seat containing a Coke, a PB&J, and in case the fish were hungry, an extra slice of bread. *You would love it here, Mama. The simplicity, the*—"Watch it!" I plastered myself against the MG as a black Dodge pickup whipped into the next parking space, getting way too close.

"Where you headed, Miss Eisenhower?" the driver yelled before coming to a complete stop.

Tanned, dark hair, brown eyes, firm square jaw…"Quinn?"

"Didn't know if you'd recognize me out of the water." He opened the door and hopped out. "You just get here?"

I glanced around, looking for others who might be members of his group.

"Jump in." He motioned me toward the truck. "There's been a change in plans."

Was he nuts? Did he really expect me to go off with someone I'd only briefly met? Not to mention the fact he stood at least six feet. "What kind of plans?"

"Come on. I'll explain on the way."

My fingers gripped the brown bag, squashing tonight's supper, but finding their way around the Coke can, my only real weapon. "I don't think so."

"They're waiting for us at Janie's."

"Well, they'll have a long wait." My gut instinct would not be ignored. With my other hand, I fumbled with my purse and found the car keys.

As I turned to leave, Quinn grabbed my wrist. "Hold on."

Visions of being held, struggling until I escaped, swirled before my eyes like a broken newsreel. I jerked away, hands curling into fists as I instinctively prepared to fight. "Don't you *ever* touch me," I spewed through clenched teeth.

Quinn's eyes widened. He held his hands close to his chest, palms out. "Hey, I'm sorry. I didn't mean to frighten you."

"'Could be you haven't met the right people. We're just plain, honest, hardworking folk.' So you said, right?" My voice trembled. "Liar."

"I didn't lie."

"Then what happened to the boat? Or the people?" I motioned toward the lake, careful not to take my eyes off him. "Where are they?"

"We had a problem with one of the motors. Travis, who's more mechanically inclined than the rest of us, tried for over an hour to fix it but couldn't. That's when Janie decided to move the cookout to her place."

"*Really?*" I snatched the fallen purse strap back to my shoulder.

"It's true. Look, the other day when we met, I thought you could use a friend...."

"How thoughtful," I mocked.

"What if you follow me in your car? That way—"

"No." His pitiful look of innocence did nothing but rile me further.

"Why? Because it's so much easier to think the worst of everyone you meet? I said I'm sorry. What else can I say or do to make you change your mind?"

"Nothing."

Silence drug out for several long seconds, neither of us willing to break the impasse. The confused look on his face—furrowed brow, pursed lips, hurt puppy-dog eyes—made him appear...innocent? I glowered before turning away, a warning to keep his distance.

"Wait," he spoke softly. "Please."

I froze as he returned to his truck. He scribbled something on the back of a card then handed it to me. "It's Janie's address. In case you change your mind." Then, without another word, he left.

For the next twenty minutes, I drove around town, too disappointed to go back to the empty cabin and angry with myself for letting down my guard. I'd been taken in by Quinn's homeboy act the first day we met—or was it an act?

Making a U-turn, I pulled into a Gulf service station, parked, and got out. I couldn't explain it. Didn't understand it. But *if* there was a cookout and *if* a person named Janie really did live at the address Quinn had given me, I had to know. And I'd need a map.

It didn't take long to find the place—an apartment building. The faint draw of music and laughter drifted through the night air as I approached the front walk. My stomach tightened. What if it was nothing more than a group of guys drinking and living it up? I stepped closer. At the sound of a female's voice, I pressed the doorbell.

A petite blonde, dressed in a tropical-print romper, opened the door. "Can I help you?"

"Are…are you Janie?"

"No, the name's Susie, but just a minute." The girl yelled over her shoulder, "Janie, someone's here to see you."

For a second, suspicion clouded my thoughts, but I'd come this far. "Actually, I'm looking for Quinn. Is he here?"

"He sure is. You must be Mamie." She swung the door open wider. "Come in."

"No thanks." I backed away from the stoop and any potential prying eyes. "I'll wait outside."

How could I face these people? No doubt, they'd asked Quinn questions. The Susie girl knew my name. Had he told them about me freaking out? Like I was insane?

Maybe I was crazy. After all, a rational person wouldn't show up at a stranger's house without a backup plan. But I was pacing in front of this girl's home, my mind a complete blank. How could I ever explain my earlier behavior or why I came?

"Mamie?"

I froze, too ashamed to look in the direction of Quinn's now-familiar voice.

"Glad you made it," he spoke without the slightest hint of anger or scorn.

Determined to apologize and leave as quickly as possible, I met his gaze. The lump in my throat took a bit of doing, but I swallowed it down and drew a deep breath. At the exact moment the words *I'm sorry* passed my lips, laughter roared from inside the apartment.

Had they been listening all this time? Were they laughing at me?

"The girls were trying to decide which game we'd play tonight,"

Quinn explained as if able to read my thoughts. "Guess they started without us. Before we go inside," he shoved his hands into his pant pockets and braced against the door, "I'm the one who owes you the apology. I had no right to grab you or expect you to jump in the vehicle with a complete—Whoa!"

Quinn stumbled, caught off guard when the door suddenly opened. He fell backward into what appeared to be Janie's living room.

"Are you all right?" A brunette with the Farrah Fawcett hair leaned over him.

He laughed as he hopped to his feet again. "I just have one question." Quinn pointed at me. "Does Mamie look like she packs that kind of wallop?"

"Quinn! You know that's not true." But he just stood there, laughing, while his friends clustered around giving me the eye. "I didn't—"

"Of course, you didn't." A girl with a head of black curls wilder than mine gripped my elbow and led me into the kitchen. "Coke, Pepsi, or tea?"

"I can't stay."

"Why? Where else do you have to be?" She filled a glass with ice. "Besides, we could use another girl in our corner. The guys are ganging up on us. How good are you at charades?"

"Never played."

She shrugged. "No problem. You'll catch on."

Elizabeth was right, I did catch on and didn't make it home until after midnight. I had not laughed so hard or enjoyed myself so much in…ever.

The next morning, someone banging on the front—and only—door of the cabin woke me. I threw off the sheet, scrambled to my feet, and tiptoed to peek out the window. "Elizabeth?"

She spotted me. "Come on. Let me in."

My hands shook as I fumbled with the deadbolt, sure something awful had to have happened after I left last night.

"Hurry up. We don't have much time."

Before I got the door unlocked, the blonde—what was her name?—Susie joined Elizabeth on the porch, both of them pushing inside.

"Much time for what?" I asked, though neither answered right away.

Finally, Susie removed her hand from her mouth. "She doesn't have a TV."

Elizabeth turned to me with her eyebrows furrowed, causing a V-shaped wrinkle in her otherwise, perfectly smooth olive complexion. "Where's all your stuff?"

Telltale heat tingled up my neck, into my cheeks. "On a wish list in the bedroom."

"You poor girl," Susie whined, adding more syllables to *girl* than I thought possible. "What do you do at night without a television?"

Elizabeth peeked into my bedroom. "I'm more concerned about how she sleeps without a bed."

"Did you two come over here at the crack of dawn to wake me up so you could snoop around? Maybe see if I'm worthy of your little social group?"

Elizabeth rolled her eyes. "'Course not." She sauntered over and pulled my hair back with her hand, then held it on top of my head. "Nah, not a good look for you. Use a headband or something to get it out of your face."

"What's going on?" I asked, a little put out with her rudeness…or was it honesty with way too much energy behind it?

"C'mon and get dressed. And make it fast. We don't have a lot of time." Elizabeth spun me around, aimed me toward the bedroom, and gave me a push. "Put on something nice. You never know who you'll run into."

"What?"

"Try to hurry." Elizabeth nudged Susie out the door. "We'll be waiting in the car."

Chapter 8

Elizabeth flipped up the sun visor and punched the gas pedal as the stoplight changed colors. "We're running behind schedule, but it's okay. We've still got plenty of time."

"Time for what?" I gripped the armrest and braced as she sped past the next light and headed out of town. "You still haven't told me where we're going."

"To the most wonderful place you can imagine, full of the best memories and happy times. Right, Susie?" Elizabeth tipped the rearview mirror. "Susie!"

The tone of her voice and the look on her face—along with Susie's lack of response—tightened my chest. I turned completely around, my knees resting on the passenger seat, and reached for Susie's hand as Elizabeth pulled onto the side of the road.

The contents of Susie's purse lay scattered in her lap. She mopped sweat from her face with a handkerchief balled up in her fist. "I can't—"

"Hang in there, Susie." Elizabeth searched through her purse, and then picked up mine and tossed it at me. "Look for hard candy, gum, anything with sugar."

"Why? What's wrong with her?" I frantically searched for something I knew didn't exist.

"She's diabetic."

Elizabeth rummaged in the glove compartment. Still nothing. She jumped out of the car, ran toward the back, and opened the trunk.

Scrambling from the car, I followed close behind. "Shouldn't we take her to the hospital?"

"She'll be all right." With confidence, she removed a box. "Get in and help me get some of this down her."

"What is it?"

She didn't bother answering, so I ran to the opposite rear door and slid in next to Susie. Strands of her wet hair plastered against her forehead.

Elizabeth sat on the other side of her, the box she'd removed from the trunk already opened. I glimpsed a beautiful cake decorated with *Happy Birthday Memaw*. Who was Memaw? Then, with two fingers, she plucked one of the pink roses and gently cradled her friend's chin with her other hand. "Here you go." She smeared a small bit of the frosting against Susie's lips. "Come on, honey, open up."

Susie obeyed her coaxing and remarkably, two roses later, the shakiness began subsiding and she regained coherency. She grabbed Elizabeth's hand. "I'm so sorry." Trembling lips matched her quavering voice.

"Nothing to be sorry about. You'll feel better once we get some decent food in you. We're almost at Papa and Memaw's. Won't take us but a minute." Elizabeth looked at me and backed out of the car, leaving the boxed cake on the floorboard. "Stay back here with her."

I nodded, thankful Susie had somewhat recovered, but nervous and still unsure of what had happened.

Within seconds, we were back on the road. Soon gravel crunched beneath the tires as Elizabeth took the next right through the opening of a split-rail fence with yuccas clustered on either side. We passed a large pond, its surface mirroring the patches of tall grass. A small flock of white geese, along with two green-headed ducks, stirred the water's smooth surface as they swam to the opposite side, announcing our intrusion.

Elizabeth pulled into the circular driveway and parked before a two-story white house with a massive wraparound porch. She nodded toward the dark-blue Volkswagen Rabbit. "Looks like Janie beat us here."

By the time we helped Susie out of the car and approached the red-bricked sidewalk, Janie came around the corner of the house with an armload of yellow-bell and dogwood branches. "Hey, girls. What took y'all so long?"

Elizabeth pointed a finger above Susie's head. "We had a wee bit of a problem, but everything's okay now."

"I saw that," Susie snapped. "I'm not blind, you know. And y'all don't have to keep hanging onto me like I'm some kind of invalid."

Elizabeth snickered. "Alrighty, then." She let go of her friend and jogged up the steps. "Because in less than two hours, we're having a birthday party, and we've got a lot to do before church gets out."

I eyed all three girls. "Will somebody please tell me what's going on?"

"My sweet grandmother turns eighty tomorrow, and we're throwing her a surprise party. And you, my dear, are here to help."

"But—"

"No buts." Elizabeth unlocked the front door, placed her hands on my shoulders, and pushed me into the foyer. "Now, let's get to work. You can start by fixing an omelet and toast for Susie and making sure she eats every bite of it. Oh, and a glass of milk. The kitchen's down there." She gestured to the right of the hallway. "I'll bring in the stuff from the car."

Elizabeth gave orders to Janie as Susie and I made our way

through the dining room and into the kitchen. I scoped out the refrigerator. "Is she always so bossy?"

Susie reached past me and slid the carton of milk from the door. "She doesn't mean anything by it. More of a mother hen, really. She and her family are very close, especially her and Memaw. That's her father's mother. They almost lost her last year. A heart attack. But she fooled them all. She—My hair!"

I spun around. Susie stood in front of a cupboard, the glass of milk in one hand, picking at her hair with the other. It took me a moment to realize she was seeing her reflection in the door's etched panes.

"What's all the fuss?" Elizabeth set a box on the counter.

"Look!" Susie screeched. "I'm a complete mess. Why didn't one of you tell me?"

"Nothing a curling iron and hairspray won't fix." Elizabeth guided the distraught girl to the breakfast table. "Now, sit down here and drink your milk while Mamie whips you up a couple of eggs to counteract all the sugar I fed you."

"The cake!" Susie busted out bawling. "I ruined Memaw's cake."

I shoved my head into one of the cabinets, looking for a frying pan, wishing I could crawl in and close the door behind me, or better yet, beat myself senseless with it. These girls undoubtedly didn't require a full night's sleep to rejuvenate their energy level, nor—in spite of Susie's emotional outburst—feel as awkward and out of place as I did.

Though the day began chaotically, Memaw's party went off without a hitch. Elizabeth had seemingly been successful in both surprising and pleasing her grandmother.

"You girls spoil an old woman." Memaw hugged each of us as we gathered the last of the things Elizabeth ordered us to place in her car. "I'm very blessed to have so many delightful young people in my life. The more, the better." She smiled at me.

After I met Elizabeth's family, it became clear where Elizabeth's bossy-biddy attitude came from. Not that her parents or grandparents displayed the trait, but the way they made over their only child and grandchild…the girl was rotten.

A hint of jealousy kept niggling at me. I couldn't help but wonder what it would have been like to have grandparents dote on my every move and word, to be showered with love.

"Are you girls leaving without telling me bye?" Elizabeth's grandfather ambled into the kitchen. "Who knows how long it'll be before I'm fortunate enough to be surrounded by so many lovely young ladies at one time."

I stepped back and eyed the old coot, whom I'd seen hug and kiss his granddaughter more than a few times today…and her him. The whole thing creeped me out.

He stopped beside his wife and slid his arm around her waist. "You girls have helped make this a special day for my Marybeth, and for that," he kissed his wife on the cheek, "I'm very grateful."

"Oooh." Susie moaned and brushed at her eyes. "That's so sweet."

Janie touched the old man's hand. "It made our day just seeing the smile on your pretty wife's face." Then she leaned over and kissed *him* on the cheek.

I tightened my grip on the box I'd been holding and used it as a shield to prevent the old geezer from moving into my comfort zone, if he became inclined. "We better get this stuff in the car."

Elizabeth peeked at her watch. "Yep, y'all better get going. Janie, Susie, I'll catch up with you two later. Mamie, thanks again for helping out."

Did she mean it the way it sounded? As if I'd been dismissed, no longer included in their little group, but simply a workhand?

On the drive into town, I sat in the back seat of Janie's car and listened to the two girls laugh and bicker, arguing about everything from who shot JR to who'd make a better president, a peanut farmer from Georgia or an ex-movie star—now the governor of California. I envied them—Elizabeth, Susie, and Janie. They'd grown up together. Probably knew each other's fears, weaknesses, and deepest secrets. I'd never known a friendship like theirs. Probably never would. I leaned back as we neared my road. For a moment, at the party, it was nice pretending.

"Wait." I twisted around for a better look. Was that...? "Stop the car." I gripped the door handle. "Janie, stop the car!"

She slammed on the brakes, sending the Volkswagen sideways in the road. "What is it?"

The swirling dust surrounded me as I got out and ran toward the trees where I'd spotted the two tow-haired children.

"Brent?" How could he and his sister disappear so quickly? At the edge of the trees, I roamed further into the woods, scanning the area, listening. Grass rustled. Wind moved through the branches. And somewhere an agitated squirrel chattered.

Janie and Susie's shouts echoed behind me, both calling my name. "Brent? Please answer."

Only silence, and still no sight of the child whose face I'd been unable to forget since he wandered into my cabin, hungry, dirty, barefooted, and—worst of all—living with a monster.

I gave up and retraced my steps, this time mindful of possible tarantulas skittering along the forest floor. Why were these two precious children more fearful of me than the dangers lurking in these thick woods?

"Who were you looking for?"

Before I could answer Susie, her eyes widened, and her hands flapped like a bird attempting to take flight. "You've got a tick on you," she squealed.

"Where?" I jumped back inside the car and frantically searched my arms and the front of my dress.

"There." She pointed toward my head. "In your hair."

"Well, get it out," I ordered on the verge of panic. "Before it gets so tangled in this mess I'll have to shave my head to find the thing."

"Eeeww! I can't." Susie swirled toward Janie. "You do it."

"You two belong in an asylum." Janie calmly twisted in her seat. "Lean forward so I can get a better—There he is." She held something between her thumb and index finger, rolled down her window, and flicked what I hoped was *it* out. "What were you doing back there anyway?"

I scratched every square inch of my scalp, imagining an infestation of bugs. "Hoping to talk to two kids I met a few days ago."

"*That's* why you ordered me to stop? You couldn't just go by their house?"

Anger mingled with embarrassment scorched my face. "You wouldn't understand."

"If it called for traipsing in the woods, you're right," she smirked, "I wouldn't."

"Even if that person, or persons, desperately needed help?"

"Were they bleeding, screaming for help, or listed as missing?"

"No, but—"

"Then what makes you think they're in trouble?" She twisted back around and put the car in gear. "Besides, any mother who'd…"

Her prissy, judgmental attitude had my dander up, and her words tuned out. What had happened to the upbeat, friendly girl I met last night and worked beside at Elizabeth's grandmother's?

Susie squirmed in the front seat, the tip of her finger a mauve color from the continuous twisting of a strand of hair.

"Let's just drop it," I interrupted. "I'm sorry I asked you to stop and sorry for upsetting everyone. It won't happen again."

"I should hope not." Janie huffed. "Why if I saw some crazy woman jump out of a screeching car and run my direction…" She shook her head. "I don't blame them. I would've run, too."

"If only I could," I mumbled under my breath, sick of her chastising.

Janie peered at me in the rearview mirror. "What did you say?"

Surprised she heard me and more than ready for this conversation to end, I smiled and answered, "I said, I probably would."

Chapter 9

Janie had hardly backed out of the driveway when I noticed it—the right front tire of my MG flat as a flitter. My fingers itched to give into anger and sling my purse against the porch. Instead, I went inside to change clothes, hoping the spare had plenty of air.

Elizabeth drove up just as I tightened the last of the four lug nuts. "Hey, girl, what *are* you doing?"

"What does it look like?" I brushed my hands together in a feeble attempt to remove the road grime, and then shielded my eyes to get a better look at what she pulled out of her car.

"Wish you would've waited until the guys got here."

A rush of panic shot through me. "What guys?"

"Come give me a hand, will you?"

I stomped toward her, hoping upon hope she didn't mean who I thought she meant. "Elizabeth....What guys?"

She handed me a cardboard box and swiped her hand across my right cheek. "What a mess. You've got dirt all over the side of your face, and look at your shirt."

"Never mind what I look like." Pure irritation laced every word. "What guys?"

"Quinn and Travis."

"Why? And what is all this?" I shifted the box and flipped a corner of the pile of multicolored fabric Elizabeth held.

"I have a wonderful surprise."

"Yeah? Well, I don't like surprises, so how about you do some explaining?"

"You'll love this one." She headed for the cabin. "Accessories to make this place a little more homey. Travis and Quinn are bringing the big stuff."

"Stuff? Are you kidding me?" I widened my strides to keep up.

"You'll have a bed, nightstand, small chest for your clothes, a sofa, and—to Susie's delight—a TV. But first, we need to get these curtains hung." She tossed her load inside. "I'll go grab the hammer and rods, and we'll be in business."

Embarrassed—no, humiliated—I didn't attempt to disguise the hot anger festering. "Of all the gall." I blocked the doorway and shoved the box back in her arms. "I may not have, in your opinion, much when it comes to the finer things in life. Never have, really. But you're not about to make me one of your little personal projects."

Elizabeth shook her head, sending a long, springy, charcoal curl loose from her updo. "That's not what this is about. Honest."

For a moment, I almost apologized for the pain—or was it disappointment?—turning the tip of her nose and her eyes red.

She set the box next to the mound of fabric. "Look, I realize I can be a little overbearing at times...."

"You think?"

"...And I know we don't know each other very well, but how could I know about you sleeping on the floor and not do anything about it?"

I lifted my chin. "I get by."

"I know you do." She flashed a dimpled smile. "All the stuff in my car, the items Quinn's bringing, they're things Memaw and

Mama no longer use. Things I hoped you could use until you get a little more settled."

"I'm sure you meant well." I clipped each word, still so mad I could spit.

Her smile faded. "Let me ask you something. Today when Susie got in trouble with her diabetes, did you feel sorry for her? Or did you want to help?"

"What kind of question is that? Of course, I wanted to help."

"That's all we're doing, Mamie—me, Memaw, Mama, even Quinn and Travis. None of us feel sorry for you, and we sure don't want to belittle you. Besides, I couldn't bear the look on Mama's face if the guys have to haul that bed back into her house. She's hated it since my early teen years when I caught her gone and hauled the thing to the garage and gave it a fresh coat of paint. Sprayed it bright red and added canary-yellow stripes for an extra splash of color. When Mama saw it, she had a fit. Said it could stay that way until the Second Coming for all she cared. Well, it seems now she cares."

"Mm-hm."

"No, really. Why do you think she sent the wild, multicolored floral bedspread and matching curtains? She hates it. All of it. So you have to take it. If not for me, for…" She broke into an Italian accent. "The ma-ma."

I bit down on my lip, refusing to let go of my anger. "I don't have to laugh."

"Come on, Mamie," she pleaded. "Why are you being such a pain?"

"Me?" I planted my fists on my hips. "Elizabeth Daniels, you are the most stubborn. Bossy. Buttinski—"

"Best friend you'll ever have." She smirked, so sure of herself.

We stood in silence. Neither of us budged. Nor blinked for what seemed like a full minute while I gathered my thoughts.

What was it about this girl? "I'm sure I may regret this—after all, I haven't laid eyes on your juvenile piece of artwork—but I can certainly understand your mother being exasperated with you. After all, I've only known you a few days, and you're driving me nuts. Okay." I threw my hands up, giving in.

She exhaled. "Good. Then it's all settled." She nodded toward the front door. "Now, how about we get busy?"

We'd hardly finished unloading her car when the guys arrived.

As soon as Quinn stepped out of the truck, Elizabeth crossed her arms. "What happened? You lose the address or what?"

"You want the long answer or the short one?"

"It doesn't matter." She waved her hand. "Back in here and let's get everything unloaded."

"Yes, ma'am." Quinn flashed a teasing grin Elizabeth's direction, and then winked at me.

My stomach knotted as prideful emotions clawed to the surface. At that moment, I felt as poor as Mr. Billy James, an older guy from Clarksdale who made his living with a hoe and shovel.

"Poor as a starving dog with the mange," Daddy used to say about him.

The dear man didn't own a car. Walked everywhere. I never saw him when he didn't have at least one, if not two holes in his shoes.

I wiggled my right great toe peeking from the tip of my ratty, lace-up Keds.

"Where do you want this, Mamie?" Travis gripped one side of the cherry-stained console TV. Quinn held the other side.

Elizabeth pointed to the far corner. "Put it over there. Looks like plenty of antenna wire poking through the wall. One of you boys can hook it up later."

Within minutes, Quinn and Travis had the truck unloaded. In less than thirty, every item set exactly where Elizabeth ordered—even the hideous iron bed.

"There." Elizabeth rearranged the throw pillows on the couch. "Now, you two guys go finish changing the flat on Mamie's car."

"There's no need for that," I insisted. "It's already done. Just have to put everything back in the trunk."

"Mission accomplished." Travis pulled keys from his pant pocket and jiggled them over my head. "That's the biggest nothing of a jack I've ever seen."

Quinn stood at the sink washing his hands. "Don't know how far you'll get with the spare. It's not in the best shape, and I'm afraid there's no fixing your flat tire. What'd you run over, anyway?"

I threw him a dishtowel. "Don't have a clue."

"Sister," Travis flopped down on the couch, "with a three- maybe a four-inch gash in the sidewall, I'd think you'd know. You should've heard it, and that baby would've been flat almost instantly."

"We scanned the driveway for the sharp culprit. No glass, metal, rock…nothing." Quinn finished drying his hands.

Elizabeth nudged Travis's knee with hers. "Go wash up before you get everything in here filthy."

He popped up, sported a wicked grin, and held his arms out. "Oh, come on, Bethy. Don't I get a hug for all the hard work I've done?"

"Get away from me, Travis." Elizabeth backed away. "I mean it."

He turned my direction. "How about you, sweetheart?"

My face flamed hot. I cringed at the thought of him touching me, even if he was kidding.

Quinn tossed the drying cloth on the counter. "Leave her alone, Travis."

But Travis didn't back off. Instead, he crouched and moved closer.

Quinn clamped a hand on Travis's shoulder. "Knock it off."

"Okay." Travis jerked free. "What's with you? I'm only teasing."

"Yeah, well, not everyone appreciates your sense of humor. Besides, we've got to get going."

"Thanks." I glanced at Quinn as I scooted past the guys and stood close to Elizabeth. "For bringing over…everything…and…" I sputtered as if suddenly plagued with some sort of speech impediment, knowing Quinn knew firsthand my fear of being grabbed.

"No problem." Then he looked at Elizabeth. "See you tonight? Or are you girls planning on skipping church again?"

"We'll be there," she answered.

We? Maybe she would. But God and I had an understanding. Besides, I'd had enough for one day, and it was time for *all* of them to leave. And this was one battle I intended to win.

Chapter 10

All proud of myself for standing my ground with Elizabeth and exhausted—more mentally than physically—I poured a glass of milk, ready to try out the TV when I heard them. Voices. Children's voices.

"What if she's asleep?" one of them whispered.

"The lights are on," came the unmistakable voice of the child who'd stolen my heart.

When I swung the door open, the two darted from the porch and headed for the hedgerow.

"Brent. Don't go." I started after them but stubbed my bare big toe. Determined not to let them get away, I hobbled forward. But it was useless. I lost sight of them and my balance and sprawled face-first at the foot of the steps. I closed my eyes. *You couldn't wait for them to knock. No, you had to jerk the door open and scare them half to death.*

"Is she dead?"

My eyelids flew open. "Brent!"

The little urchin squatted on his hands and knees, staring into my face.

"Where's your sister?"

His stubby finger pointed to my left.

I rolled over and sat up. "What are you two doing out this time of night?"

"We snuck out to tell you something. Didn't we, Lily?" The adorable freckle-faced child didn't wait for his sister's response. "But you cain't tell nobody."

"About you sneaking out or about what you want to tell me?"

"Both." Lily glanced in every direction as if she expected the devil himself to appear. After my run-in with Aaron, I knew the frail child had just cause.

Burning pain shot through my toe when I attempted to stand. "Lily, you and Brent run inside and wait for me. Shut the door and turn off the porch light in case someone drives by."

Lily reached for her brother's hand and took off like a flash, careful not to let the screen door slam and quick to follow my instructions about the light.

Holding my breath, I gave the sliver of wood embedded under my nailbed one quick jerk. I had to remind myself to breathe while fighting the urge to throw up.

Again, I pushed myself up and then limped inside the cabin.

"Your toe, it's bleeding." Lily shot off the couch.

"You want to get me a towel?" I nodded toward the bathroom. "And wet the corner of it, so I can wipe the blood off before it gets on the carpet."

Brent stood next to me, twisting his little fingers together. "Does it hurt bad?"

"Nah."

As soon as Lily handed me the towel, I wrapped it around my foot and hobbled into the living area while Brent clutched my hand and grunted as if he held all my weight on his tiny body. He waited for me to get settled before he crawled on the couch beside me, practically sitting in my lap.

"How'd you two sneak away without Aaron and your mama knowing? And why?"

"Aaron ain't home."

"He's *not* home, Brent."

"That's what I said." He furrowed his brow, obviously confused by his sister's correction.

"Where is he, and what about your mom?"

Lily sat on the floor with her knees pulled to her chest. "Aaron went to go play poker with some of his buddies."

"On account he and Mama got in another fight."

"Hush, Brent," his sister scolded.

"What kind of fight? A yelling fight or a hitting fight?"

Lily stared at the floor. "I can't say."

"Mama cried."

Lily leaned forward and glared at her brother. A look that had him squirming. A look that had me convinced Lily fully understood the consequences if caught breaking their silence.

"It's okay." I reached for Brent's small hand. "I won't say anything."

Lily began to rock back-and-forth. "You know this afternoon when you saw me and Brent, and we ran?"

"Yes."

"We were afraid you might be mad at us."

"Why? For what?"

"On account of your tire," Brent blurted. "Except, we didn't do it."

I glanced at Brent, then Lily. "How did you know about my tire?"

"Remember… You said you wouldn't say anything. Not even to the police. Promise?" Lily chewed on her thumbnail. "He'd know if you were to tell."

"Who? Aaron?"

The two nodded.

"Me and Lily followed him this morning and hid in the bushes.

He had something in his hand, and he squatted beside your car." Brent's eyes widened as he held his little fist in the air and slammed it down hard on the palm of his other hand. "And stabbed the tire like they show when a bad guy kills the good guy on television."

I shuddered at the visual. "What time this morning?"

"Sometime after you'd left," Lily answered.

"Since the car was here, how would you or anyone else know I wasn't?"

"Because we heard Aaron talking on the phone. He said, 'She's gone, you say?' Then he said something about," Lily swallowed, "'wait till she sees what I do to that fancy, little, red car of hers.' And then he laughed and hung up. Since you've got the only little red car around here, when he started out we followed him."

"Who was he talking to? Do either of you know?"

They shook their heads. But only Lily spoke, "No, ma'am, but you forgot to promise you wouldn't tell. You've got to promise!"

"Ain't no woman ever gonna talk to a man disrespectful and get away with it," Aaron had boasted the day I threatened to call the police when he drew his hand back to hit Brent. "Around these parts," he'd snorted, "we don't threaten unless we got something to back it up with." And without Lily and Brent, I had no real proof.

Deep breaths did little to douse the fear sparking through my veins, nor the pity for the fear I'd seen on their faces. "I won't tell." The words hardly left my mouth before I wished I could take them back. To not say anything to the authorities made me as weak and guilty as their mother and allowed Aaron to continue to go unpunished for his actions, but somehow, I had to gain Lily's and Brent's trust.

Lily sprang to her feet. "We got to go."

"You're right. Let me change clothes, and I'll drive you partway."

"No!" Lily snagged Brent's arm and jerked him off the couch. "Somebody might see and tell."

Brent clutched Lily's hand with both of his. "Aaron's gots lots of friends. Mama says people are watching us and her all the time, and they tell him everything."

"I know you and your mother are afraid of him. But if your mama would stand up to him. Let some of us help her…"

"She can't." The fear in Lily's eyes spoke louder than her words. "He says if any of us ever tell anything, he'll make us wish we never did."

"What if I take you and your mother someplace where Aaron will never find you?"

Lily shook her head. "He would."

"No, I promise you he wouldn't. You'd be safe."

Lily tugged her brother toward the front door.

"Maybe I could talk to your mother. Tell her I want to help."

"She'd be awful mad if she knew we were over here and said anything." Lily, with Brent in her grasp, rushed out into the night and disappeared, leaving me rubbing the goose bumps from my arms, reliving some of my own nightmares.

Somehow, I had to find a way to keep those two safe.

Wide awake, I flopped over to check the time—2:24. Less than thirty minutes had passed since I'd last looked. I couldn't stop thinking about Brent and Lily. Or the monster who lived with them. Lights on or off, it didn't matter, visions of Aaron had flashed before my eyes almost nonstop since the two little ones left me standing on my front porch, worrying if they would make it home safely.

"Hump!" I pounded my overstuffed pillow with my fist in an attempt to make a more comfortable spot for my head. "Home? Safe?" Meaningless words in their world. Or mine after the tire incident.

Why had I promised I wouldn't say anything? The thought of

keeping my mouth shut stirred an anger teetering on the verge of rage, while going to the authorities screamed traitor and possible harm to two innocent children.

I threw the covers back, tired of fighting for sleep. Perhaps another glass of milk. Or perhaps… I paused in front of the older black-and-white TV Travis hooked up earlier, pulled out the small button on the front, and twisted the large numbered knob. All those channels and nothing. Nothing but static and gray snow or a blank screen. Strange. Did all the networks really think the whole world went to bed after a certain hour?

Exhausted, I braced my hands against the shower wall as shampoo suds streamed down my back like gentle fingers—loving, caring. A mother's touch. Soothing to my throbbing head. How I missed her. But she was gone, and nothing would ever change that.

When finished, I turned off the water wishing I could crawl back in bed. The linoleum floor cooled beneath my feet as I reached for another towel and wrapped it around my wet hair.

"Mamie?" A voice that sounded much like Quinn's came from the front porch, along with a knock.

I scrambled into my faded, blue cotton robe and dashed to the front room. When I opened the door, Quinn leaned back against a porch post with his arms folded across his broad chest.

"Good morning." He stood there, every hair in place, crisp white shirt, khaki pants, polished boots, and that smile.

A blue jay squawked overhead as if mocking the uncomfortable moment of silence and my gawking.

"Why are you here this time of morning?"

A hint of gold—or perhaps a spark of mischief—lit his brown eyes. "It's a long walk to town."

"What?" I looked in the MG's direction.

"Don't worry. Your spare held up overnight." He pushed off from the post. "But if I were you, I wouldn't try to get too many miles out of the thing."

He'd driven out here just to check on me? To make sure I wasn't stranded?

"In fact, there's a shop, Big R, downtown that'll probably have the size tire you'll need, and they'll do right by you."

"Thanks."

He nodded. "No problem." Then he started to walk away and stopped. "You like seafood?"

What a strange question. "Yeah."

"Good." He smiled and sauntered toward his truck. "I'll pick you up at seven."

"What?"

"And dress casual," he yelled, right before he slammed the driver's door and started the engine, not giving me a chance to refuse or even tell me where he purposed to take me.

"Wait."

He smiled again, waved, and backed out of the driveway.

"Wait!" My sore toe protested as I stomped my bare foot against the porch. "Of all the nerve." I whirled around and limped back inside. Just like a man. But *this* man made me feel things I'd never felt before—all jittery inside, confused, exuberant...and riled.

"Don't be a fool, Mamie. A few acts of kindness don't make a hero." *Even Dad played nice when he wanted something.*

Chapter 11

Pain radiated from the base of my neck to the top of my head. The flickering fluorescent light overhead and the smell of raw meat and burning plastic wrap only intensified it.

"Mamie," Dave bellowed.

"What?"

He pointed the tip of his knife toward the deli. "Better get your mind on work."

"Sorry. I didn't hear the bell."

"Yeah, right. Suddenly, you've gone deaf?"

"If only it were possible." I wiped both hands on my apron and hurried out, desperate to escape Dave's continued ranting.

"There she is." Mrs. French smiled. "How are you, dear, and how are things at the cabin?"

I thought about the tire in my trunk. The one I'd been assured couldn't be repaired. The one replacing would cost me almost every penny I had. "Fine."

"No problems?"

"Nothing to worry about." But I was worried and had a whopping headache to show for it. "What can I get you?"

"Let's start with a pound of liverwurst. No, better make it two. It's my husband's favorite. Of course, you must know that by now."

I slid open the meat-case door, pulled out the stinky loaf Jim referred to as poor man's pâté, and placed it on the slicer. "Yes, ma'am." A cat would be hard pressed to eat the stuff. "The usual thickness?"

"Please. And better give me a pound of ham and a half pound of Pepper Jack. Just leave the packages on top when you're done." She tapped the metal case with her pencil. "I've got some other things on my list to get."

"Mrs. French?"

She halted. "Yes, dear, what is it?"

"I was wondering. Did you get my money order…for April's rent? I mailed it early."

"It came Saturday." She nudged her half-glasses further down on her nose. "Are you okay, Mamie? You look tired."

"Do I?" My voice exuded peppiness. "Can't imagine why." Between worrying about Brent and Lily and what Aaron might pull next, who could sleep?

"Is Harry—Mr. Aldridge—working you too hard?"

"No, ma'am."

"Good." She pushed her buggy forward. "And don't you let him."

"Yes, ma'am."

I moved the blade lower, flipped the switch, and began slicing her order. I tried to think of something pleasant. But the same thoughts and worries consumed every spark of brain matter in my aching head. Who told Aaron about me leaving yesterday and why? Had Brent and Lily made it home safely? Without getting caught? What if their mother asked for my help? I'd promised Lily I would take them someplace where Aaron couldn't find them, but where? And as if I didn't have enough problems, Quinn expected me to have dinner with him tonight, and I still hadn't settled on a tactful excuse yet. But tactful or not, it wasn't about to happen.

———⟨⟩———

"Sorry, Quinn, I can't go out with you. It's been a long day. I'm tired, my head hurts, and I wouldn't be good company. You're a great guy—handsome, smart, kind. Most girls would give anything to get to know you. But let's face it, sooner or later you'll end up like all the other men in the world…one big, mule-headed jerk."

I jabbed a finger at my reflection in the mirror. "Maybe you should leave the jerk part off." My stomach rumbled as if protesting the rudeness that would lead to yet another PB&J sandwich. I had to admit the steady diet of the same-old-same-old was wearing thin. Maybe there wouldn't be any harm in enjoying a decent meal…just this once?

An engine's roar and gravel crunching beneath tires expedited my decision.

A plain, white peasant dress hung in the closet next to my favorite jeans. I snatched a lime-green T-shirt from its hanger, shoved my arms through the shirtsleeves, yanked it over my head, and then reached for the pants.

But what if he's wearing slacks and a nice dress shirt? My heart rate kicked up a notch. I hesitated and gave the dress a second look.

A knock on the door left no time for fence straddling or last-minute primping. "Coming." I zipped my jeans and raced to open the door.

Quinn's earthy, after-a-rainstorm scent drifted in. He stood on my porch with his thumbs hooked in his pants pockets. His *denim* pants. "Ready?"

I took a deep breath to calm my nerves. "Let me grab my purse."

"You won't need it." His smile widened. "Not where we're going."

"What's that supposed to mean?" I placed both hands on my hips, prepared to unleash the words I'd practiced before the mirror but with a lot more attitude.

"I thought you might feel more comfortable if we had supper here."

Panic overruled good manners. "Here? No!"

"Wait. Let me show you." Quinn sprinted toward the truck he'd backed into the front yard at an angle. He dropped the tailgate with a loud thud and lit a lantern. Within seconds, he removed two lawn chairs and a cooler. Red coals from a hibachi glowed in the breezy night air.

The screen door slammed behind me. "You're going to cook? Here?"

"I promised you dinner, didn't I? This way, you get dinner and a live show." He motioned toward the sky.

The small strip of a moon tilted on its side, giving the surrounding stars little competition for light.

"Mamie, say something. If you'd rather go into town—"

"No. This is perfect." The darkness would hide any moments of awkwardness. After all, I'd never dated, never been alone with a guy before. "You just caught me off guard."

"Sure?"

"Um-hum." I walked out to the grass, hugging my chest.

"Cold?" Quinn flipped the lid back on a wooden box. "Here." He removed a blanket and draped it around my shoulders, his fingers brushing the bare skin on my arms. His touch set off a different type of chill. "How about some hot chocolate, or I've got Coke, Dr Pepper?"

"Maybe later." I settled in one of the chairs. It seemed he'd thought of everything. Made me wonder how many women Quinn wooed with his charm and night-under-the-stares routine. "Can I ask you something?"

He busied himself removing items from the cooler. "Shoot."

"Why are you being so nice to me?"

He set a Tupperware bowl on the tailgate and faced me. "What kind of question is that?"

"You don't even know me. I mean, I'm sure you've got other friends—girls—who you've known most of your life."

"Yeah."

"So?" I leaned forward, determined to get an answer.

"Don't you know most guys are intrigued by a beautiful mysterious woman? Somewhere underneath all that red hair and hurt lies the answer. All I know is I like you: your smile, innocence, even the spitfire temper. And I want to get to know you. Really know you."

I stood. The blanket slipped from my shoulders. "You mean other than a friend? Because that's all I want. A friend. Nothing more."

Quinn reached for me. Then he hesitated as though he thought better of it. "Relax, Mamie. It's not like I asked you to marry me or have plans on making some type of improper advances toward you."

His words left me speechless.

"Here." His mouth twitched. "How about some hot chocolate? It might warm you up?" He handed me a steaming cup.

But I was no longer cold. My face still burned. Probably glowed brighter than the coals in the Hibachi he'd carefully placed on the edge of the tailgate.

"Hope you're hungry." Quinn grabbed another Tupperware container from his cooler as if nothing had happened. "I couldn't decide between potato salad or slaw, so I got both. Didn't know if you preferred shrimp or scallops, so…" He held wooden skewers packed with the two choices, stacked between chunks of mushrooms, onions, and bell peppers, and laid them on the grill.

I gripped the cup with both hands while he sprinkled each kabob with generous amounts of Old Bay seasoning. "Looks good," I muttered, still trying to figure this guy out.

Within seconds, a pungent, but wonderful smell permeated the air. Too bad humiliation put a dint in my appetite.

Quinn glanced over. "How was work today?"

"Fine."

"Got your tire problems taken care of, I see."

I sipped from my cup and nodded. Great, we'd now resorted to small talk. Next, we'd be discussing the weather.

Several minutes passed without a word. Finally, Quinn broke the silence. "Looks like these babies are almost done. You wanna grab a coupla of plates and utensils out of the box?" He pointed toward the crate he'd retrieved the blanket from earlier.

"Sure." No problem, since the sooner we ate, the sooner this little cookout could end. But did I really want to spend the rest of the night throwing up raw fish? I walked over for a closer inspection. "Are you sure they're done?"

"Oh!" He stepped back, holding his chest. "It's bad enough the lady questions my intentions, now she insults my cooking."

"No, it's not that. It's just—"

"I'm messin' with you, Mamie. But to answer your question, I'm sure."

I chewed my bottom lip and tried to come up with some sort of apology. "About earlier...I'm—"

"Don't worry about it. Frankly, I'm flattered. I planned this whole shebang—the meal, a night under the stars, all of it—to impress you. In hopes we *could* be friends. Had my speech all ready when you jumped up and announced—how did you word it? 'All I want is a'...?"

"Okay, okay." I turned my back to him in pretense of trying to find those stupid plates. "I know what I said."

"I hope you meant it."

My mouth suddenly went dry.

"Well?"

As if my tongue had been tied in a knot and shoved down my throat, all I could get out was a barely audible, "Um-uh."

He tapped me on the shoulder. "Was that a yes?" A hint of laughter laced his voice.

"Yes!" I swirled toward him, scattering paper napkins inside the truck bed and on the ground. "But *only* friends."

"Without friendship, what else *can* there be?" This time, not the slightest hint of teasing colored his voice or twinkled on his face. Only those kind, piercing, brown eyes twisted my insides in ways I'd never before experienced.

My heart stuttered. At a loss for words, I scrambled to collect napkins before the soft breeze cast them across my front lawn.

By the time I'd captured them, Quinn had set two plates stacked high with food on the TV trays before our chairs. He gestured toward one of them. "After you, my lady."

So formal, so polite, so strange.

He took his seat next to me and bowed his head. "God, I thank You for a beautiful day, a perfect night, and my new friend, Mamie. May this food nourish our bodies and this meal be one of many we enjoy together."

I peeked at Quinn. His head remained bowed, his eyes closed. *One of many?* Not hardly.

Chapter 12

A layer of chocolate coated my tongue. How many S'mores had I eaten? My stomach pressed against the now-tight waistband. Another bite of anything, and the snap on my jeans would pop on its own. "I can't remember the last time I roasted marshmallows."

Quinn reached for the graham crackers. "I hoped you'd enjoy it. I think it's one thing you never get too old for."

"Everything was delicious, the shrimp and scallops… Who taught you how to cook by the way?"

"The same ones who teach us all, I guess. Our moms and grandmothers."

"It just seems odd, you being a guy and all."

He arched an eyebrow. "No worse than a woman knowing how to change a tire, is it?"

I tried to wipe the stickiness from my hands. "Touché."

"An older brother or your father?"

"Excuse me?"

"Who taught you how to change a flat?"

"My dad. He wouldn't allow me to drive without knowing how."

"Yeah, fathers are like that, aren't they? So protective of their little girls."

I drew in a ragged breath and didn't comment.

"Are you the oldest, youngest, or—"

"An only." Somehow, I needed to change this topic.

"No fooling? Bet it was hard saying goodbye."

"More than you know." I shook my head, not wanting to relive the night of Mom's death, but the memory played on.

"She's gone," the nurse spoke softly.

Mom's breathing stopped, but the arteries in her neck continued to pulsate slow, yet steady. I begged God to help her. When the nurse tried to cover Mom's face with a sheet, I pointed out the lingering sign of life.

"It's a natural reflex. Sometimes the heart continues to beat for a very short while, even after the patient's respirations have ceased."

"Please." My heart raced trying to escape the pain. "Can't you do something?"

The young nurse, not much older than me, pulled the stethoscope from around her neck, adjusted the earpiece to her ears, and placed the metal disc to Mom's chest. But the pulse in Mom's neck had stopped.

"...Mamie. Mamie!" A warm hand touched the side of my face.

I jerked away. More out of habit than fear.

Quinn frowned and dropped his hands to his side, confusion twisting his face. "Are you okay?"

Would I ever be? I wadded up a napkin and mopped the tears from my face.

Quinn handed me his handkerchief. "I'm a good listener, if you want to talk about it."

I didn't, but he deserved an explanation for my odd behavior.

"Mamie?"

"My mama's dead." I'd not said the words out loud since those predawn hours when Dad finally came home in a drunken stupor. He'd shown no emotion, just stared at me, and then walked away.

Something inside me wanted to punch him in the gut, make him feel a fraction of my pain. "She died two weeks ago tomorrow."

"Man." Quinn made a half turn, then faced me again. "Me and my big mouth. I'm so sorry."

"You didn't know."

"Two weeks? And in that time you moved and started a new life?"

"Without Mama, I had no reason to stay in Mississippi."

"So your dad…he's…?"

"Dead?" I mocked laughter. "Not unless he's killed himself driving drunk or some woman's husband finally caught up with him."

The muscle in Quinn's jaw twitched. Obviously, he didn't know what to say, and I'd already said too much.

"It's late." I handed him his handkerchief, then picked up the blanket and began folding it. "We better get all this stuff packed and put away."

His hands stilled mine. "I can't tell you how sorry I am for all you've been through."

"Thanks." I forced a smile. "And thanks for dinner." I wanted to say something more, like the night was special—and to my surprise, it had been—but I didn't dare give him the wrong impression.

Chattering birds awakened me to a new morning. I lay in bed and listened, testing my knowledge, identifying the different species—the hoarse cawing of crows in the far distance, the ever-present blue jays with their calls of alarm, a mimicking mockingbird, and the cheery robins.

For the first time in weeks, I'd awakened happy, almost giddy. Full of joy…full?

Last night wasn't a dream. Quinn, the cookout on the front lawn, my fill of chocolate. All real. And fun and… I pulled the covers over my head. And *stupid*.

I slammed my fist against the mattress. Why did I have to mess it up by crying and telling him about my mother's death? Even the contentious feelings for my dad spewed from the depths of my soul.

What was I thinking? Worse yet, what was he thinking? Probably walk, don't run to the nearest exit? Guys didn't want to hear that kind of stuff or deal with a blubbering female—friend or not.

If only life were full of do-overs. But it wasn't. With a grunt, I uncovered my head, tossed the sheets back, and scooted out of bed. Although once again sad and lonely, I was still employed. Which meant one thing: get up and get going.

I showered quickly and skipped breakfast. I was in no mood to eat now. Besides, who could be hungry after how much I'd eaten last night? By seven forty-five, I pulled into M&H's parking lot. Grinning. Dave would have a stroke. Me, fifteen minutes early? Couldn't wait to see the look on his face. The door slammed behind me, but Dave was nowhere in sight. Only Jim, and he had his back to me with the phone pressed to his ear.

I smiled and waved when he glanced over his shoulder.

"You need what?" Jim practically screamed into the receiver. "And if I find it, you want me to—" He turned again and looked at me, his eyes wide. "You can do that?… Okay, I'll look for it and call you right back."

"Look for what?" I surveyed his expression as he stood with the phone still in his hand. I'd never seen him stand still. "Jim…? Look for what?"

He finally hung up. "Dave's finger."

I laughed and headed for the back room. "Sure."

"I'm serious, Mamie, and I could use your help."

"Nice try." Refusing to fall for his shenanigan, I didn't slow my steps. "In case you haven't noticed, my hair's red, not blonde."

Still tying my apron, I entered the market, ready for work.

Jim stood at Dave's workstation picking through beef chunks, eyeing each one carefully. "Could you at least check on the floor?"

So he did think I was stupid. But two could play this game. "Which one are we looking for, the thumb or the pinky?"

"The tip of his right index. The nurse on the phone said if we could find it, there's a good chance the doctor can sew it back—Wait!" Jim stopped his search and eyed something in his hand. "Come over here and see what you think."

My mouth went dry. "You're kidding, right? I thought you were kidding."

"No." Jim took a step toward me, holding out something in his palm. "Does this look like part of a fingernail to you?"

I shaded my eyes with one hand while gripping my stomach with the other. "Don't!" My heart pounded as though it might explode. "I mean it. Don't you dare come near me with that thing." A bead of sweat dripped from my forehead and trickled down my right temple, the room so hot I couldn't breathe.

"I just thought with both of us looking… The nurse said time was—Mamie?"

Jim's voice drifted a million miles away. My body swayed. Then everything went black.

The next thing I knew, Jim was kneeling beside me, trying to explain to Dave. Dave? But it can't be. He was at the hospital. This couldn't be. I looked at all the stainless-steel cutting tables, the band saw, the grinder, the chrome handle on the walk-in cooler.

"Look," Jim interrupted my survey. "She's awake."

"Get out of the way," Dave ordered Jim as I began to sit up. "Let me help you, Mamie."

His stubby fingers gripped my upper arms and pulled me to my feet. My stomach quivered at the thought of his bloody, partially amputated finger against my skin.

"Mamie, I'm so sorry. I didn't think you'd—"

"You're right," Dave barked. "You didn't think. Next time you get some crazy notion to pull a prank like that, it better be on the other side of these walls." Dave waved his right hand toward the back door.

His right hand. I looked closer. Every one of his fingers remained fully intact. I peeked at his left hand and inspected it as well. Not as much as a hangnail.

"Mark Twain had it right," Dave continued his rant. "'The first of April is the day we remember what we are the other three hundred and sixty-four days of the year.'" He leaned forward and stared straight into Jim's eyes. "Some of us anyway."

I glared at Jim. "This was your idea of a joke? I could've broken my neck falling on this concrete floor. For crying out loud, are you nuts?"

Jim's look reminded me of an old basset hound Dad had years ago. "I really am sorry. Let me get you some ice for the lump on your head."

"No." I stomped my foot, too angry to care what size knot protruded from my forehead. "I want to know who you were on the phone with when I came in. Obviously, it wasn't someone from the hospital."

Dave folded his beefy arms across his chest and waited for Jim's answer.

"A customer. But wait." Jim directed the comment to Dave, whose face instantly turned scarlet. "Hear me out."

Dave unfolded his arms and stepped toward Jim. "You better talk and talk fast. You can start by telling me *which* customer? So help me, if you've—"

"Let me explain," Jim interrupted. "Mike, from Sassy's, was finishing his order when I heard the back door slam and saw Mamie. I *waited* for him to hang up before pretending to be talking to a nurse from the hospital."

Dave muttered something under his breath, spun on his heels, and began pacing, never moving more than three or four feet away.

Jim eyed me and mouthed, "I'm really sorry."

Fully convinced he was only minutes away from losing his job, I nodded and mouthed back, "Me, too." As angry as I'd been earlier, I couldn't imagine working here without Jim.

The pacing finally stopped. I held my breath and wrung my hands, waiting for Dave to say something.

He stared at Jim, his look stern. "I'm going to have to let you go."

Jim's shoulders slumped. The color drained from his face.

"But…but I'm okay." I rubbed my hand across the walnut-size lump above my left eye. "It's just a bump on the head. Really. I'm not even mad anymore. Please—"

"April fool!" Dave sputtered with laughter.

My mouth fell open. I'd never heard Dave laugh. Thought him incapable of doing anything other than barking orders and wearing a permanent scowl. I peeked at Jim. He stood with his mouth partially gaped open, speechless.

"Well?" He slapped Jim's shoulder. "How does it feel when the jokes on you? Not so funny, is it?"

"You mean I'm not fired?"

Dave slipped between us. "Did you learn anything?"

"More than you know." Jim held out his hand. "Thanks, man."

I stood almost dumbfounded. To think the guy I'd thought heartless and uncaring was capable of being…human. I eased closer to the men. "Yes, thanks, Dave."

"Are you sure you're okay, Mamie?" He eyed me.

"I'm fine. Really." I just bashed my head against the concrete floor and wished I'd not gotten out of bed this morning. But other than that…

"Then can we kindly get some work done around here?"

Dave's scowl had returned, as well as his gruffness, but now, he looked and sounded different. I'd gotten a glimpse of the real Dave. The one Jim had been trying to tell me about all along.

"What's going on in here?" Mr. Aldridge smiled from the doorway.

I whispered only loud enough for Dave to hear me while pulling strands of hair from under the hairnet. Just enough to help cover the small goose egg. "Think I'll go to the break room and put some ice on my head."

Within five minutes, max, Mr. Aldridge pulled out a chair and sat next to me. "Let me take a look."

"It's nothing."

"I'll be the judge of that," he spoke firmly, but his face shone with kindness. I pulled my hair back. He gently touched the injured area. "Maybe you should see a doctor."

"No, sir. I'm fine." Other than my brain's about to burst through my scalp.

"I don't mind my employees having fun, but I don't approve of what Jim did. He's smart, witty, and a hard worker, but I won't tolerate antics that cause harm."

"But—"

He held his hand up. "Jim assures me he's learned his lesson, and I trust Dave when he says the matter's been taken care of. My only concern now is you."

"I'm okay. But if you don't mind, could I keep the area covered? You know with my hair. Just until it clears. Curious minds will lead to questions at the deli counter."

He patted my hand then stood, ready to leave. "If it makes you feel more comfortable. But you know." His eyes twinkled. "We could always have Jim work the counter as part of his punishment."

I smiled up at him. "I'll keep that in mind."

"I'll check on you later." And with that, Mr. Aldridge left. Leaving me to brave a relieved sigh and ready, as Dave would say, to—"Get to work!"

By noon, my head hurt something fierce. Not so much from the morning's fall, but the grumbling from my midsection reminded me I hadn't eaten breakfast. Thoughts of a thick, chocolate milkshake teased my appetite. Until last night, I'd gone weeks without the one flavor I craved more than any other. Now, like an alcoholic tumbling from the wagon, I had to have more.

Jim recommended Wally's. Even drew me a map.

I drove slowly, watching for the landmarks he'd written down. That's when I saw him…Quinn holding open the driver's door of a white Firebird for a tall, slender young lady. Platinum-blonde hair—teased and lifted to perfection—practically swallowed her face. But her do, like her clothes—straight-leg jeans and neon-pink T-shirt—screamed style.

Quinn leaned in and kissed her, then wrapped her in his arms.

Emotions stirred inside of me. Emotions I refused to spend time analyzing. After all, what was he to me…a mere acquaintance, nothing more than a friend—if that?

Mortified at the thought of being seen, I waited for the traffic to clear and headed back in the opposite direction, my craving for chocolate gone.

Chapter 13

Jim and Dave had worked nonstop all morning. Saturday, and still orders poured in for tomorrow's Easter feast—rack of lamb, prime rib, and ham. Lots of ham, both shank and butt cut. Before M&H, I never knew the difference.

With each long day, Dave's fuse grew shorter, and Jim grew quieter. My mood wasn't much better. Since the cookout Monday night, I hadn't seen or heard from Quinn. I'd felt…I heaved the bin of meat onto the counter, unable—or was it unwilling?—to clarify how I felt.

Ding, ding, ding, ding, ding.

The deli counter bell announced yet another impatient customer. The week had been full of them. A few complained, most boasted about having their children all together again. I couldn't help but wonder what it would be like to sit around a table with brothers, sisters, grandparents, and Mom surrounded by all her family, laughing—really laughing. Or a dad who loved his family more than he did his next drink.

Ding, ding, ding.

I cringed and tossed my latex gloves in the trash, the lack of patience now surging through me as well. "Coming," I announced in the best upbeat tone I could muster.

Ding. Ding-ding.

Impatient? No. This person was downright rude, thoughtless, and—"Elizabeth!"

Her perky smile slid into pursed lips and widened eyes. "Girl, please tell me they don't pay you to wear that ridicules garb on your head."

My ears felt as if they'd self-combust with shame, especially when I noticed Mrs. Owens, only a couple feet away, eyeing us while randomly picking up canned products—none of which made it to her buggy.

"And that apron. Is this someone's idea of one size fits all? If not for the ties, you'd be swimming in it." Elizabeth plastered herself to the meat case and stood taller. "You *are* swimming in it. The thing practically drags the floor."

"Elizabeth, please." I scanned the aisle to see who else might be witnessing my dressing down…literally.

"How many of the guys back there," she motioned toward the market, "wear hairnets?"

"They don't," I whispered, hoping neither Dave nor Jim had tuned into our conversation.

"And why not?" she practically shouted. "Are they bald?"

Elizabeth was pushing the envelope and my hot button. "Would you please keep your voice down?"

"All I'm saying," she lowered her tone, "if they're not, then I don't get it."

"The Health Department—"

"Yeah, yeah." She rolled her eyes. "I know all about the hair thing. But hair's hair. Short, long, what difference does it make? No one wants it in their food."

"Will you stop it? I don't need you to tell me how homely I look in this getup, but I'm lucky to have this job. And quite frankly, if it called for it, I'd wear pink hip waders to keep it."

Elizabeth busted out laughing. "I believe you. But the point is, you don't have to. Check out some of the other stores in town. Their gals wear their hair pulled back or up and some of the cutest little scarves. There's no reason you can't do the same. Tell you what. Why don't I grab a pizza and come by tonight? We can play around and come up with something that doesn't scare all the eligible bachelors away."

"First of all, I'm not looking for a man. Second of all…" A picture of the fashion queen in the white Firebird popped into my head. Who was I fooling? Even though a man wasn't on my agenda, I needed all the help anyone had to offer. Besides, I'd tell her anything to shut her up. "Sure."

"Alrighty, then. I'll see you tonight…say six thirty?"

"I should be home by then."

"Great." She turned to leave.

"Elizabeth?"

"Yes."

"Didn't you forget something?"

She furrowed her brow. "I don't think so."

I tapped the top of the metal case. "Sandwich meat, cheese?"

"Nah." She waved me off with her hand. "I just stopped by to see if you wanted to go out to eat or take in a show or something, and thankfully, I did. You're a mess." She laughed. "But not to worry, you're in good hands. There's nothing I can't fix, given enough time and the right hair products. You'll see."

"What type of products?"

"Don't worry. I've got it covered. Meanwhile, call whichever laundry service y'all use and have them swap out some of those Amazon aprons for a few petite ones. I mean it," she called over her shoulder. "And be assertive. Don't take no for an answer."

There must be a fine line between assertive and just plain bossy. Whichever the case, Elizabeth had 'em both down pat.

"Yow!" I rubbed the crown of my head. "That hurts."

"Sorry." She picked up another hunk of hair, turning my curls into a ratty mess. "But haven't you ever heard that looking your best is worth a little pain? Why, I knew a woman once who wore nothing but size six AA shoes. Had a real flair for fashion and always claimed to have such dainty feet that she had to go all the way to Little Rock to buy her shoes."

"So what's your point?"

"Point is, she didn't wear AA, but she pulled it off. For years, she crammed her fat feet into those tiny shoes. Made it all the way to her sixties before vanity took its toll. Of course, a combination of arthritis, broken bones, and bunions didn't help any. Now, the poor soul can't wear anything but house shoes, even to church."

"And the moral of that story is what? Forty years from now there'll be a whole generation of women with heads slick as a baby's bottom from all the hairspray, teasing, coloring, and permanent-waves?"

"Will you quit your complaining and pay attention so you'll be able to do this yourself. We're almost done. You just need a little more height on top so when I pull it back you won't look so…dated." She reached for a crocheted, green hairnet thingy she called a snood. "Heard Quinn made you supper the other night."

"Who told you that?" I huffed. Both of us making eye contact with the other's mirrored image.

"The cook. How was it?"

"It was okay." And that's all you're getting out of me. "Why do they call it a snood and where'd you find it anyway?"

"I have no idea where it got its name. Memaw made this one for me several years ago. Says they've been around since the 1500s but became popular during WWII. A real fashion statement. They'd trim them with beads, bows, and feathers—He said y'all cooked out."

I turned my head and made direct eye contact. "No way am I wearing feathers." And no way am I going to tell you anything concerning Quinn, the cookout, or the fashion queen with the platinum-blonde hair.

"Will you be still." She handed me a mirror.

"Shhh." I grabbed her arm. "Did you hear that?"

Neither of us moved.

"There it goes again." I sauntered to the bedroom door with Elizabeth close behind me.

"Someone's on the porch," Elizabeth whispered. "It can't be Janie or Susie. They're both out of town."

It couldn't be Brent and Lily. Not with Elizabeth's car in the driveway. "The guys?"

"I wouldn't think so. They'd be pounding on the door by now."

"Unless they're wanting to scare us." In the kitchen, I mouthed, "On the count of three." With my hand on the doorknob, I held up one finger, then two. On three, I jerked the door open.

A high-pitch scream pierced the night air, and in a flash, the child took off running.

"Lily, wait! Lily, please come back. We didn't mean to scare you."

"Who is she?" Elizabeth asked.

I didn't have time to explain. Instead, I leaped from the porch and ran after her, pleading for her to stop. Something was bad wrong. Why else would she be out this time of night?

Without streetlights and with the clouds obscuring heaven's lights, it was useless. If Lily didn't want to be found, she wouldn't be. I bent over catching my breath. "Lily...honey...it's Mamie. I can't run...anymore." I listened. Nothing. "I know you can hear me. I'm not going anywhere. I'll sit right here. The rest of the night if that's what it takes. See?" I crossed my legs and eased to the ground while imagining ticks, mosquitoes, and snakes all around, yet I was too concerned for Lily to care.

I didn't have to wait long. The crackle of a breaking stick unnerved me at first. Then I heard a child's voice a few feet away. "Where's that other woman?"

"Her name's Elizabeth, and she stayed behind."

Lily stepped through the bushes.

"Would you like to go back to the cabin and meet her?"

"No! I won't talk to anyone but you."

"Okay." I spoke soft and calm while my imagination ran rampant. What had Aaron done to frighten such a sweet child? To cause her to come to me for help, someone she hardly knew? "You want to tell me what happened?"

She didn't answer.

"Did Aaron do something?"

She whimpered at first. Then her small shoulders began to shake with uncontrollable sobs.

I reached out and pulled her to me, her tears soaking into my blouse. Anger surged through me, an all-too-familiar anger, at the thought of a man's vile hands on an innocent child.

"He hurt him bad."

"Who, Lily?" My heart raced. "Brent? Where's Brent?"

"They took him to the hospital. Told me to stay put. Said if anybody asked, to tell them he fell down the stairs. But he didn't. He didn't, Mamie!" Again, she wept.

"Shhh." I breathed into her ear, trying to comfort her while dealing with my own fear and anger.

"Mama and Aaron were fighting. Brent stood on a kitchen chair next to Aaron and told him to leave her alone. Aaron laughed and slid his foot next to the chair leg and flipped it over. I tried to catch him, but couldn't. He hit the table then landed on top of the fallen chair.

"He didn't cry at first. He didn't make a sound, like he couldn't breathe. Then he took in a big gulp of air, held his stomach, and cried. Aaron kicked him and told him to stop his whining and to get up. Aaron's always saying Mama and I baby him too much and it's time for him to grow up and be a man. But he's only five."

"Then what happened?"

"Brent's face went all white. That's when Aaron acted all nervous. Told Mama to wrap him in a blanket and get him in the truck. All I know is they took him to the hospital. But, Mamie." She grabbed my hand. "I'm afraid. What if my little brother never comes back home?"

"Mamie?"

Lily stiffened at Elizabeth's voice and pulled away, wiping her face with the neck of her T-shirt. "She can't find us."

I gently held Lily's shoulders. "Look at me."

Even though it was dark, I searched the outline of her little face close to mine.

"You're going to have to trust me, Lily. You're a brave young lady, who's a little afraid right now. But I need you to trust me. Can you do that, even if it means trusting my friend?"

Elizabeth called out again.

Lily jerked away. "I've got to go."

"Lily, wait!"

Chapter 14

"Elizabeth, stop!" I stood out in the road where she could hopefully see me waving my arms or hear me. "Don't come any further."

"Mamie, what's wrong?"

"I need you to run back to the cabin, get my purse, lock up, and bring your car. We're going to the hospital."

"Is it the little girl? You? Tell me what's going on."

"Elizabeth, please, just do what I said. And hurry."

As soon as I heard Elizabeth racing down the road, I walked back to the edge of the woods. "I know you heard me, Lily. My friend, Elizabeth, and I are going to the hospital to check on Brent. If you want to go with us, it's time to stop acting like a scared rabbit and come out of hiding. It's time to be that brave little girl who came to the cabin earlier tonight. The one who had the courage to tell me what *really* happened to her little brother."

"Why does *she* have to come?" Her voice sounded only steps away.

"Because you're a child. And they probably won't allow children in the hospital this time of night. Besides, when Aaron sees you, what do you think will happen?"

"I don't care," she all but screamed, her words bathed in anger.

"Sure, you do. And if I go in to check on Brent, Aaron will be equally as mad. Plus, he'll know you told me, won't he?"

"I guess." Her voice dropped barely above a whisper.

"But if Elizabeth goes in and Aaron sees her, he won't think anything about it."

"How's she going to find out anything? She doesn't even know my brother."

The glare of what had to be Elizabeth's headlights dashed toward us. "We'll figure out something. We don't have all night to stand out here and talk about all the what ifs. You have to make up your mind to trust me or not."

Elizabeth pulled up beside me and rolled down the window. "Which one of you is hurt and how bad?"

"We're both fine."

"Then what in blue-blazes is going on, and why the big rush to get to the hospital?"

"Because someone we know and love is there. Isn't that right, Lily?" I reached and opened the back door. "The sooner you get in, the sooner we can make sure Brent's all right."

"Who's Brent?"

I looked at Elizabeth and shook my head slightly, in hopes she'd not say another word.

Lily came out of hiding and, staring at Elizabeth, stood by the opened door. Then finally slid across the back seat. Fearful of her changing her mind and making another fast getaway, I slipped in next to her and closed the door.

Elizabeth turned on the overhead light, stretched her arm across the back of the seat, and twisted to look at us. I supposed to satisfy her curiosity that we were both truly unharmed.

Lily had already ducked down on the floorboard.

"Turn off the lights, Elizabeth."

"What's wrong with her? Why's she down there?"

"She doesn't want to chance anyone seeing her. Now, kill the lights."

"Okay." The inside light went off. "But I don't know who you think might see us." Elizabeth scanned the outside surroundings. "There's no one around here?"

"She's afraid and for good reasons."

Elizabeth finally put the car in gear and headed down the road. "You two have sure got me confused. You're off to the hospital to check on some guy named Brent."

"It's not some guy." Lily crawled out of the floor and snuggled up next to me. "He's my brother," she corrected with all the moxie of a protective big sister.

"Well, pardon *me*…Lily, is it?"

"Um-hum. I mean…yes, ma'am."

"Tell me, then. If you're so afraid someone might see you, how to you propose to walk into a well-lit hospital—even if they'd let you in? You're a bit young, you know?"

"She's not going in."

Elizabeth looked at me in the rearview mirror. "Oh, I see. Well, unless you can convince someone you're a family member, they won't be letting you in, either. Look at the time. Visiting hours are over."

"They might possibly make an exception. Maybe for someone who has connections? Like a well-known hometown girl."

"Me?" The car fishtailed and jolted to an abrupt stop. She slammed the car in park and twisted around in her seat. "You think *I'm* going to waltz right in there, ignoring all the rules, to check on Lily's brother when a phone call will suffice?"

"I asked you why she had to come." Lily's voice cracked. Then came the tears. "I knew she wouldn't help." She reached for the door handle close to her. When I grabbed her hands, she scrabbled toward the opposite door. I put my arms around her and held her close. Her little fingers tugged on mine. "Let me go! Brent needs me."

"Lily, calm down. Listen to me," I pleaded.

"What on earth." Elizabeth's voice hissed barely audible over Lily's ranting. "That child has a major problem."

"She sure does." My gaze bored through Elizabeth's. "It's called emotional and physical pain, fear, lack of trust, and no one to protect her. Her world consists of a man who beats her mother and God only knows what he does to Lily and her brother. Her brother's in the hospital, hurt. How bad? Who knows? This little girl asked for my help, and I'm going to give it to her." The words had spewed out in anger. Misdirected anger. I closed my eyes and took a slow, deep breath in an attempt to regain my composure before uttering the words, "I'm sorry."

Lily had stilled in my arms. I stared out the side window into the dark of night, not daring to blink for fear the pooled tears would fall.

"Shouldn't we go to the police and not the hospital?"

Lily began physically shaking. "Why did you have to tell her? He's going to be mad. He'll kill me. He'll kill me," she kept repeating in a fit of near hysteria.

"No!" I rocked Lily, assuring her I wouldn't allow anyone to hurt her. A promise I might not be able to keep.

Elizabeth eyed me for the longest minute, then asked, "What does this guy she's so afraid of look like? I'll also need his name and Brent's last name."

"You don't have to do this, Elizabeth. I've got a plan."

"Yeah, what?" Elizabeth passed a wad of Kleenex over the back seat for Lily.

"I'm sure they took Brent through the emergency room, so why can't I go in pretending to be sick with…I don't know…sore throat, appendicitis, back spasm, something?"

"And when you don't have a fever, or better yet, insurance, what will you do? Did you think of that?"

There it was, that always-present, take-control, bossy tone of hers. "I guess not."

"Well, I did, and like you said, I've got connections. *If* the right people are on duty."

By the time we made it to the hospital, I didn't know who was more nervous, me or Lily. "I hope my brother's okay," she kept repeating while all kinds of questions ran through my mind.

What if Brent had already been discharged home? Wouldn't Lily's mother be frantic when she couldn't find her daughter? And if he had been discharged, how could I take Lily back to the hellhole she called home? The only hope of any real help for Lily and her brother meant she'd have to talk to the authorities and tell them the truth. With all the fear Aaron instilled in her, though, how would I ever manage that?

Elizabeth parked the car close to the emergency room and grabbed her purse. "I still need information, y'all. What does this wife-beater character look like, his last name?"

"He's a big, burly guy. Heavy set, black hair, not well kept. His last name is Holbrook. Lily and Brent's mother's name is Tammy."

Lily's eyes met mine, her face all scrunched. "How do you know my mother's name?"

"Does Tammy have a last name?"

Stunned that these children and I had a connection, yet I didn't even know their last names, I had to ask, "Sweetheart?"

"It's Cunningham. Same as me and Brent."

Elizabeth got out of the car. "Wish me luck. Don't panic if I don't come back right away. It may take me some time to schmooze my way in, to find out if either of my friends, Bridget or Shirley, are working tonight." And with that, she slammed the door and crossed the parking lot.

A siren wailing in the distance unnerved me. It reminded me of all the days and nights I'd spent with Mom in the hospital. Ambulances coming and going. How many times I'd prayed for the person, someone's loved one, to make it as I watched my mother slip away.

"Do you think Brent'll be all right, Mamie?"

"Didn't anyone ever tell you, little boys are tough as nails?"

"You didn't see him. He went so…like this." She fell back in the seat with her mouth gaping open, moaning.

My stomach tightened. I pulled her up and held her close. "Try not to think about it."

How I wanted to shake my fist, scream at God, and ask why? But He stopped listening to me a long time ago.

Lily slid to the edge of the seat and looked around. "I know. Let's play a game. I spy…something yellow."

"I'm afraid I don't know that one."

"It's easy. You look around, spot something, and say, 'I spy something…' and then tell what color it is. When the other person guesses it, you switch."

The game went on forever, but it took Lily's mind off Brent when all I could think about was what was taking Elizabeth so long? She'd been gone for over an hour.

"I spy…Hey, look! It's your friend."

Elizabeth jogged to the car, opened the door, and jumped in.

Lily leaned over the front seat to bombard Elizabeth with questions. "Did you see my brother? Is he okay?"

I tugged on Lily's waist. "Sit back, honey. Give her a chance to catch her breath."

"I didn't see your brother. He'd already been admitted to the pediatric unit, but my friend, who works on a different floor, was able to find out some information for me. They're running some tests."

Lily twisted the amethyst ring on my finger. "What kind of tests?"

"Some type of scan on his abdomen…his stomach. Don't ask me what for, because I don't know anything more."

Elizabeth's eyes, so full of intensity, locked on mine. She patted at her neck. "My necklace, I've lost my necklace. I bet it fell off when I was running." She opened the glove compartment and retrieved a flashlight. "Mamie, you've got to help me find it."

"I can help, too."

"No," Elizabeth said, her tone bossier than usual. "Aaron might come out and see you. I think it's best if you stay in the car."

Once Elizabeth and I got out of the car, she scanned the pavement with the flashlight. "I didn't lose a necklace, but act like you're helping me look anyway and listen up. The cops have been called. The doctor didn't buy the story of Brent falling down the stairs. Something about the bruising…I couldn't keep up with it all. They think he may have a ruptured spleen."

"What does that mean?" I touched her arm. "Is it serious?"

"According to my nurse friend, yes."

"Bad enough he could die?" My heart rate increased, threatening to choke the life from me. "Is he going to die?"

"Mamie, get a grip." Elizabeth tugged on my arm and crouched onto the pavement, taking me with her. "She said it was serious, not life-threatening. I don't know about these things. My friend warned me that if I knew something and was holding back information…well, you get the gist. From the way she talked, I'm thinking this isn't the first time Aaron has been accused of abuse. Like it or not." Elizabeth positioned the light, making it easier for us to see one another clearly. "We could get into some real trouble here. Lily's got to tell the authorities what happened. For her sake and ours."

"Did you find the necklace?" Lily called out.

"I'll need some time alone with her," I whispered.

"Take all the time you need, I think I'll go have another nasty cup of hospital coffee and hang out in one of the waiting rooms. Thirty minutes be long enough?"

"Yeah." I stood and headed toward the tow-haired angel hanging out the window, concerned about a make-believe necklace.

Chapter 15

The wide-eyed youngster scooted over as I slid in next to her.

"Did your friend find the necklace?"

"Lily…" How do I tell her?

She looked over my right shoulder. "Is she going inside to hunt for it?"

I cupped the little girl's thin face with my hands. "Sweetheart, we need to talk about Brent. Aaron hurt him bad."

"But you said he'd be okay." Her chin began to quiver. Soon tears rolled unchecked from squinted eyes—eyes no longer focused on me.

"He will be," I whispered into her ear as she buried her face against my chest. "The doctors and nurses are taking good care of him."

"I hate him. I don't care what Mama says. I hate Aaron and wish he was dead."

All the right things to say came to mind—how God didn't want us to hate, how we were supposed to forgive—but I hadn't finished working through that process myself. Who was I to chastise the dear child? "Maybe it'd be better if you focused on Brent getting well."

"Can I see him?"

"Not right now. Maybe in a few days. Once he gets better, we can ask about you visiting him."

"A few days?" She mopped her face with her shirt. "How long does he have to stay here?"

I searched for the tissue Elizabeth had given me earlier. "We don't know yet."

"Why?"

"Because they want to watch him, check him out real good… maybe ask him some questions about what happened."

Lily jerked away. She shook her head, sending wispy strands of white hair in every direction. "He won't tell. Not Brent."

"Will you?"

"I can't," she shouted. "You better not, either." Her fingers gripped the seat. "You promised!"

My thoughts ricocheted in two directions. How to keep her safe and how to hold her trust? "Let's say you had the power to choose whether you and Brent ever had to live with Aaron again—"

"Mama, too?"

"Your mother would have to decide for herself. I'm talking about you and Brent. And Aaron would never be allowed to hurt either of you. Ever."

"But he'd still hurt Mama."

I leaned against the seat and closed my eyes. How do I make her understand? "Lily, I'm going to tell you something that I've never told anyone else."

"Not even Elizabeth?"

"No one." I sat up straight. "Other than my mother."

She twisted around to face me.

"My father hurt me when I was about your age."

"Did he hit you?"

"No." Nausea and rage washed over me as the unforgettable scene ran through my mind once more. After a deep breath, I continued, "But what he did wasn't right, and he would have hurt me again and again except for one thing—I told someone. My mother."

"Mama already knows Aaron hits me and Brent. He hurts her, too."

"Maybe there's someone else you should tell."

Lily fidgeted with the seatbelt. "I did." She peeked up at me. "I told you."

Those soft-spoken words punched me in the gut. One wrong decision tonight would douse Lily's hope. A single wrong word would give her reason to never break her silence again. How could I protect her? I wasn't her mother, had no authority. And if the legal authorities failed her, then what?

My throat ached. The lump refused to go down no matter how many times I swallowed. "The fact that you told me, proves how very brave you are. It also shows how much you love your mama and Brent."

Her little chin dropped to her chest. "Do you think Mama loves me and Brent?" Before I could answer, Lily continued, "If she did, she'd make Aaron stop…like your mama did *your* daddy."

"Oh, Lily." I tipped her face up. "She loves you and Brent. Don't ever doubt that."

"Then why? Does she love him more?"

"What do you think?" I tapped her chest with my finger. "What does your heart tell you?"

We sat in silence for several seconds.

"Mama's happier when it's just her and me and Brent. We play games, sometimes. Go for walks. Sing. But when it's time for Aaron to be home, she makes me and Bent leave—or if the weather's bad—we have to stay in our room."

"Sounds like she's trying to protect you in her own way. By keeping you out of sight so Aaron won't hurt you."

"Sometimes he wants to find us, though. Why can't she just make him leave?"

"I used to wonder the same thing about my mama. I'd get so *mad*."

Remembering some of my foot-stomping fits as a child brought a sad smile. My hands would search for hips that hadn't developed yet, a stance I hoped made me appear more grown-up and make my words—"we don't need him"—sound more convincing.

As time passed—and hips and the rest of my body developed—the way out for me and Mama became clear in my mind. I'd graduate from high school, get a job someplace far away, and we'd move. Leave Dad and his many acts of infidelity and pain behind.

"Did she?"

The vision evaporated at Lily's voice. "What?"

"Did your mama ever make your daddy leave?"

A cluster of moths fluttered around a nearby light. "No." I bit my lip and hoped Lily wouldn't ask any more questions. "Enough about me. Tonight, we need to figure out what to do with you."

"I don't want to go home."

"And I don't want you to."

Lily bounced to the edge of the seat. "So when Elizabeth comes back, we can go to your place, right?"

"We can't."

"Why?" Her cute smile dissipated.

"Because when Aaron discovers you're missing, the cabin is where he'll come first."

The driver's door clicked. Lily screeched and I jumped.

"So are y'all about done?" Elizabeth got in and slammed the door behind her.

"Not quite."

"Did you find your necklace?"

"My—?" Elizabeth winked at me. "She's got a memory like a steel trap." Then she smiled at Lily. "No, honey, but it's okay, I've got others at home."

"Hey, maybe we could go to her house. Aaron wouldn't ever find me there."

Elizabeth's mouth gaped open. She didn't utter a single word or make a sound. Only glared at me. Speechless. But not for long. "Are you ready to be incarcerated for kidnaping? That's what could happen, you know."

"No one's going to jail." I shot back, my nerves balled in knots. At least, not tonight.

Lily gripped my arm. "I'm scared."

I pulled her close. "You're okay. We're all okay, except I bet you're hungry. How's a hamburger and milkshake sound?"

She released her grip. "Chocolate?"

I smiled and brushed sprigs of white hair from Lily's eyes. "A girl after my own heart. What do you think Elizabeth? Willy's still open this time of night?"

"On a Saturday night? Yeah. But then what?"

"I'm thinking." I'd been thinking, and the same two people kept coming to mind.

Lily's eyelids drooped. Her head bobbled. I removed the partially eaten hamburger from her clutch, wrapped it up, and moved her small body around until her legs rested, curled on the seat, her head in my lap.

"Now what?" Elizabeth whispered. "We have names, Uncle Bud and Grandmaw Murt Blaylock, but no idea where they live. How'd you know about them anyway?"

"It's a long story. But Bud and Lily's mother are brother and sister. If we can find out where they live, maybe they'd be willing to let Lily stay with them and help us come up with a better plan."

"We don't have a plan. What we need to do is go to the authorities. *Tonight.*"

"We need more time. You heard her. Lily's scared to death of Aaron. Perhaps with Bud and her great-grandmother's help, we can convince her to talk with people who will remove her and her brother from the home, keep them safe from Aaron's wrath. Maybe even bring charges against him for child abuse. Who knows, if Aaron ends up in jail, Tammy might develop a backbone."

"Well, I don't know any Bud or Murt, and without an address, we'll—Hey, look who just pulled up. It's Quinn. Bet he can help us."

"No," I demanded through clenched teeth. We didn't need to get anyone else involved. But it was too late. Elizabeth exited the car and ran over to the black pickup parked three spaces down. No doubt, that blonde beauty sat next to him, but all I could see from this angle was Elizabeth hanging on the truck door.

Quinn leaned his head out of the driver's window and waved. Embarrassed and agitated, I jerked my head in the opposite direction. "We don't need his help," I spoke softly…more to myself than to Lily, whose breathing remained slow and even.

Within minutes, Elizabeth opened the car door and climbed in. "Quinn thinks he knows the Murt you're talking about. Says his grandfather used to buy hay from Murt and her husband, Wade Blaylock. It's been a while, but he thinks he can remember how to get there."

"Great. Only one problem. Lily and I are taking up most of the back seat, so I'm afraid everyone will have to sit up front."

"Everyone? Who's everyone?… Oh, you mean Travis." She pulled down the visor and ran her fingers through her long black curls. "Quinn's by himself."

"Took his date home early, did he?"

"His date?" Elizabeth eyed me in the mirror. "What are you—?"

"Shush," I demanded and held my palm up as the front passenger door opened.

Quinn focused on Lily sleeping soundly in the back seat before his eyes met mine. "How anyone could hurt a child is beyond me. How'd you get involved in all this, Mamie?"

"If you don't mind, I'd rather not talk about it right now."

"Sure." He nodded. "Like I told Elizabeth, though, it might be easier if we went in my truck. There's a stream we'll have to cross. A lot of gravel roads."

I waited for Elizabeth's response. After all, it wasn't my car.

"Come on." She motioned for him to get in. "We don't have time to waste. By now, this Aaron character is either locked up or at home calling the police to report a missing child, who happens to be in the back seat of my car. And I'd rather she be found with her legitimate family."

"Not that I don't appreciate the help, but this is my problem. If you'll take me to the cabin and, Quinn, if you'll write down the directions—"

"Forget it," Elizabeth snapped. "We're in this together."

"That goes for me, too." Quinn eased the door shut and motioned for Elizabeth to head toward Main Street.

Within minutes, we'd left town and smooth pavement. I could smell and taste the dirt stirred by Elizabeth driving much too fast. Trees lined the road. There were fewer houses, and most of those were dark except for an occasional porch light.

"Better slow it down. Get ready to take the next right. From that point on, if my memory serves me, the road narrows and is curvier than a snake's track."

Also full of potholes he failed to mention. At spots, Elizabeth couldn't avoid hitting them. Even at a crawl, a harsh grating noise had me convinced parts were being ripped from the bottom of her car. No way would my MG have survived. Why would anyone live so far out of town?

"Whoa."

I rose in the seat to see what brought Elizabeth to a halt.

"You call that a stream?" she questioned Quinn.

The headlights sparkled off water running down what appeared to be more like a four-foot wide ditch, rather than just a dip in the road. "Now what?" I squeaked.

"I knew we should've come in my truck." Shaking his head, Quinn mumbled and stepped out of the car.

"What are you fixing to do?" Elizabeth asked.

He pulled up one foot and then the other, removing shoes and socks before rolling up each pant leg. "We'll either drive or walk the rest of the way. There's only one way to find out."

Chapter 16

Lily reached for Quinn's hand. "Are we almost there?"

"Not much farther," he assured her.

"I certainly hope so." Elizabeth slapped her neck. "These mosquitoes are relentless."

My fingers itched to scratch a few of my own bites. Instead, I focused on Lily as she talked and laughed with Quinn. She didn't appear afraid of him at all. Not from the moment she woke and I introduced her to him. Even when he scooped her up in his arms and carried her through the water, she giggled. What made her trust him after living with a man like Aaron?

A low-pitched snarl, followed by aggressive barking, jolted me. Lily's scream pierced the night air. I blinked several times before my eyes focused on a big, black, furry creature.

"Oh, Lord, save us." Elizabeth sunk her fingernails into my forearm.

I inched forward and prodded Lily until she stood tucked behind me.

"It's okay. He won't bite. See?" Quinn held his hand out for the dog to sniff.

Lily squeezed between me and Quinn. "Can I pat him?"

"No!" I insisted, horrified of her being mauled.

"Sure," Quinn answered as if I'd not said a word.

"I'm with Mamie. We're in enough trouble. All we need is to end up back at the hospital with a child—who doesn't belong to any of us, I might add, no kin whatsoever—whose arm's been bitten off by some overgrown, flea-infested mongrel."

"Where'd he come from?"

"You see the light over there?" Quinn stooped over, leaned his head close to Lily's, and pointed off in the distance. "I'm ninety-nine percent sure that's your great-grandma Murt and Uncle Bud's house. I suspect this old boy belongs to them."

"Good. Great. Now that we've got that all settled." Elizabeth stomped her feet and flapped her arms. "Can we get moving?"

We started forward, and Lily once again gripped Quinn's hand.

Seemed he attracted women of all ages. The blonde beauty. Now Lily. What was it about this guy?

I mentally slapped myself for entertaining such thoughts. After all, what did it matter?

Lily tugged on my sleeve. "He likes us."

"What?" I gasped. Had I spoken out loud?

"Him." She patted the giant fluffy shadow stalking us. "He's following us."

"Umm," I answered and willed myself not to say or think another serious thought until we reached the house now in view.

"If it is their house," Lily squealed. "There's a barn where I fed Honey and Calvin apples. That's the names of the horses. And they have chickens and cats. Do you think they'll remember me?"

"I sure hope so. Otherwise, we're all in big trouble."

"Will you stop it?" I whirled toward Elizabeth. "She's talking about the animals...I think. Quinn, this is the place, right?"

"I'm pretty sure. Hard to tell, though. You girls wait here. No need in all of us getting shot." He chuckled and headed for the house.

"Oh no you don't." Elizabeth clawed her arms. "Right now, I'd rather be shot and put out of my misery. If one goes, we all go."

We ran to catch up, the four of us traipsing through the yard toward the house. We'd almost made it to the front steps when a beam of light came on, shining in our eyes, blinding us.

"Stop right where you'ins are and state your business."

The man's stern words sounded much older, more serious than I remembered from my one encounter with Bud. But the "you'ins" caught my attention. Most of the people in Mountain Home said "y'all", same as in Mississippi.

Quinn spoke up, "We're looking for the Blaylocks."

"Folks around here—least those with good intentions—come calling in the daylight, not this time of night."

"Bud?"

The light shifted from Quinn's face to mine. "Miss Mamie?" He stepped closer and noticed Lily. "What in tarnation? Where's Tammy and Brent?" He glanced from Lily, to me and waited for the answer.

"There's been an accident."

"An accident?" He thrust his fingers through his hair and growled like some wild animal before slinging the flashlight across the lawn. For several seconds, we stood mute. Bud paced in front of us. He didn't utter another sound, as though afraid to hear any details.

A creepy squeaking noise broke the silence. Bud stopped in his tracks and spoke toward the front door. "Everything's okay, Gran. Go on back to bed."

"Don't look or sound like everything's okay," a raspy female voice responded. She flipped on the porch light. "Invite them people inside while I put on some coffee."

"You'ins go on in." Bud extended his hand toward the porch. "Me and Miss Mamie'll be on in a minute."

Lily's eyes locked on mine as if pleading to keep her secret.

"It'll be all right, honey. You go on with Quinn and Elizabeth."

Bud waited for them to reach the top step before he turned to me. "Look, I need to know before we go inside…is my sister and nephew… are they…?"

"Your sister's not hurt, but Brent's in the hospital." My throat clogged at the thought of the child who might be fighting for his life. "From what my friend, Elizabeth, could find out, he's hurt bad."

"Aaron?" The name boiled from his throat.

I nodded.

"How did it happen?"

"Lily needs to be the one to tell you, not me."

"But you'ins know?"

"For whatever reason, she trusts me. Something I gather doesn't come easy for her or Brent. And the longer we stay out here talking, the more unsure of me she'll become."

"So you'ins ain't going to tell?"

"Look, she's afraid, and why shouldn't she be? He's threatened all of them. Told them what he'd do if they ever said anything. It's not like the poor child doesn't know what he's capable of. They've all been living in fear far too long, and it has got to stop…. Someone has to tell. And personally, I think Lily's brave enough to be that someone. But right now, she needs a safe place to stay. That's why we brought her here."

"There's more than one way to stop Aaron Holbrook." Bud turned and stormed away. "And it's long past due."

"What are you saying?" I ran after him. "Bud!" I grabbed his arm as he opened the truck door. "Where are you going?"

He jerked from my grasp and jumped inside the cab.

"Bud, don't do this! Your family needs you."

But he wouldn't listen.

I stepped back as he sped away, leaving clouds of dust burning my eyes and throat.

"What's going on out here?" Quinn asked, stopping beside me. "Where's he headed in such a rush?"

For a moment, I couldn't speak. I stood dumbfounded, caught up in Lily's nightmare world. I struggled to pull myself away from the hellish acts taking place in my subconscious.

"Mamie, talk to me."

The whir of the truck's engine grew faint. "I'm afraid he might do something stupid."

"Like what?" Quinn placed his hands on my shoulders and forced me to face him. "You're afraid Bud might do what? Go after the guy who hurt Lily's brother?"

I glanced at the others standing on the porch. "Shhh. There's no sense in upsetting everyone. But to answer your question, yes."

"He's just young and upset. It's natural. Once he blows off some steam and calms down, he'll decide it's better to let the authorities handle it, and he'll be back."

"You don't understand. He told me he thought about killing him."

"He said that, just now?"

"No. He came by the cabin one day, right after I moved in. His sister sent him to warn me. About Aaron…the guy who's been living with Lily's mom. He said—"

"Whoa. What do you mean: warn you about Aaron? I didn't know you knew the guy. Or Bud."

"Please keep your voice down? Look, I only met Bud the one time."

"The day he warned you about Aaron?"

"That's right."

"And how is it you know this Aaron fellow? Did you meet him at work? At the boat docks?"

112

I stiffened and pulled away from him. "Well, it's not like I went out with the guy if that's what you're thinking."

"How do you know what I'm thinking? For crying out loud, *I* don't know what I'm thinking!"

"Stop yelling at me!"

"I'm not…" He lowered his voice and dragged his right heel through the gravel. "Did Bud have a gun? Wait a minute. It doesn't matter. We couldn't get through, so he can't get out."

"But he's in a truck."

"So? Don't you see? Elizabeth's car has him blocked off. Unless there's another way—"

"He'll be back." I finished his sentence.

"Do you two mind?"

I jumped and plastered myself against Quinn's chest, then pushed away as if I'd touched a bed of hot coals. "Couldn't you have called out or something?" I scolded Elizabeth, more upset with my actions than the fact that she'd seemed to have appeared from nowhere.

"For your information, I did. But it seemed y'all were too engrossed in some kind of private conversation. Mrs. Blaylock… Murt… is upset. She doesn't understand why Bud took off without saying anything. And, of course, her being upset heaps more apprehension on Lily. We could all use some answers."

Forty-five minutes passed and Bud still hadn't returned. Nor had we heard from Quinn, who took Elizabeth's car to try to catch up with him, once Murt confirmed there was another road leading to town.

Lily had curled up on the blue floral sofa with her head resting on Murt's lap.

"Should we put her in bed?" I asked.

"I hate to disturb her. She had such a hard time falling asleep, but it'd probably be best. We'll put her in my room. You might as well plan on staying the night. We've got plenty of space if you girls don't mind sharing a bed."

"No, ma'am. I mean…we appreciate it, but surely, we'll hear something soon." Lily didn't budge or make a sound when I lifted her.

"I hope so." Elizabeth yawned. "Mrs. Blaylock, do you mind if I put on a fresh pot of coffee?"

"Help yourself, honey. You'll find the coffee in the cabinet to the right of the stove. And please, you girls call me Murt. Mrs. Blaylock sounds too stuffy."

I followed the petite elderly woman down the hall. She held herself up straight, claiming every inch of her five-foot frame. Wispy gray hair lay limp around her shoulders. The multiple waves made me suspect she wore it up during the day.

"Here we are." She folded the covers back. "Take her shoes and those dirty clothes off. I'll get the night-light from the bathroom in case she wakes and doesn't know where she is. You'll find one of my undershirts in the top chest drawer. It'll swallow her, but it'll do for now."

By the time the child's great-gran, as Lily called her, returned, I'd accomplished only half of my mission.

"Child, why don't you let me finish up? You go join your friend and get yourself a cup a coffee."

Undressing the child was awkward. I'd be the first to admit my lack of experience with children, but no way could I abandon the old woman to do all the work.

"Don't look so guilty." Murt's bright, youthful eyes didn't fit the wrinkles etched in her face. "And don't deprive me the joy of feeling useful. Bud, Tammy, and her two little uns are all I have left in this world. I've prayed many of nights for God to allow Tammy and Lily and Brent to be a part of my life again. More than four years now. And just look." She gestured toward Lily.

"But what if He doesn't? I mean… answer the prayers the way you want Him to?"

"Child." She slipped Lily's shirt over her head. "You cain't bargain with God. And you cain't let your personal will stand in His way. You pray believing, but always knowing God's ways are best."

I drew in a ragged breath and slipped out of the room. How could my mother's death be best for me? How could an innocent child, suffering, lying in a hospital, be best for him? I stared at the empty, rock fireplace. Its upper edges smudged from years of use. Although the grate lay clean of logs and ashes, the smell of burning wood lingered in the air… much like the ache in my heart would forever be present.

"Hey." Elizabeth exited the kitchen, her hands cradling a steaming mug. "Where's Murt?"

I nodded toward the bedroom and headed for the wooden rocker I'd claimed earlier.

"You want me to get you a cup?"

"No. I don't want anything, other than Quinn and Bud to get back here."

"Is she calling it a night?"

"I don't think so."

"She hasn't asked a lot of questions up till now, but you know with Lily out of the room, that's bound to change. Have you thought about what you'll tell her?"

"The truth, I hope." Murt smiled at me from the hallway. "That always seems to work best, don't you think?"

Chapter 17

Murt deserved the truth, didn't she? But so did Lily. The poor child had been betrayed enough…by her mother, no less. By admitting to Bud that Aaron played a role in Brent's injuries, I'd already said too much.

"Did you find everything, dear?" Murt asked Elizabeth as she crossed to the sofa and sat beside her.

"Um…" Elizabeth took a sip from her mug and swallowed. "Yes, thank you. Could I get you a cup?"

"Maybe later." Murt's deep-blue eyes focused on mine. They mirrored the kindness in her voice. "What I'd really like are answers. I may be old." She laughed. "But for now, my mind's as sharp as ever, and I'm not some fragile china doll you need to protect. So let's start with Brent. What happened tonight, and how bad is he?"

I leaned back in the chair and pressed my toes against the floor, nervously sending the rocker into a slow steady rhythm. "As Lily said, he's in the hospital."

Murt crossed her legs and propped her elbow on the couch arm. "It's what she didn't say that concerns me. Her fidgeting and not looking me in the eye has me convinced Aaron Holbrook had a hand—literally—in the reason for my great-grandson being in the hospital. In fact, I'm sure of it. And all the swopping looks between you and Lily tell me you know more than you're saying. So I'll ask you again, what kind of shape is Brent in?"

Guilt gnawed at me. "I really don't know, other than what Elizabeth found out. Perhaps she could better explain his *condition*"—I emphasized in hopes she wouldn't give anything more away—"since she's the one who actually spoke to the nurse."

"Perhaps I should clarify." Elizabeth squirmed and glared at me. "I didn't speak to *Brent's* nurse. I spoke to a friend of mine." She faced Murt and continued, "A nurse who worked on a different floor. After making a few phone calls, she discovered there'd been tests run, but not all the results had come back. She assured me the doctors were being thorough, and they should know more by tomorrow."

"When Bud tore out of here as if the seat of his britches was on fire, had he been told...?" Murt's parchment-thin skin turned ghostly white. Air rushed from her mouth, and she gripped the armrest. "Is my great-grandson dying?"

My feet stiffened, bringing the chair to a halt. "No, ma'am."

The older woman eyed us. "Then what aren't you telling me? Have the two of you been told to keep me in the dark?"

"No," Elizabeth and I both answered.

"No," I repeated and scooted out of my chair and knelt before her. "Don't even think such a thing."

A faint smell of lavender and roses reached my nostril as she leaned forward. "Then tell me what *to* think?"

A moment of silence stretched between us. "I don't know." My insides churned at the lie.

"Your face tells me different."

Of course, it did. Unlike my father, I'd never quite mastered the art of deception without incriminating myself.

I wiped my sweaty palms on my pant legs. "Lily came to me. She was crying, frightened. More for Brent, I think, than herself. All she wanted was a ride to the hospital, to check on her brother."

"So you said earlier, and that explains how she ended up with you all. But you've still not answered my question, have you?"

My heart ached for the older woman. She had to be nervous; my nerves were raw. But I couldn't break my promise. "You'll need to ask Lily."

"Lily?"

I bit my lip and nodded.

"She's just a chap. Her own mama'll go to her grave protecting that disgraceful man. And if she stays with him, I 'spect he'll be the one to send her there…maybe even one, if not both, of her children first. No." Murt frowned and shook her head. "Lily'll never breathe a word. None of 'em will."

"But she already has." I spoke slowly and emphasized each word. My eyes locked to Murt's, willing encouragement into her frail heart.

Murt blinked and sat up straight. Seconds later, she asked, "Lily told you?"

"Yes." I smiled.

"It *was* Aaron, wasn't it? She told you *he* hurt the boy?"

I kept my eyes fixed on her and refused to respond.

"And you didn't tell the police?" Murt jolted from the sofa. Coffee sloshed over the rim of Elizabeth's mug as the fiery woman pushed past her, headed for the kitchen. "Then I will."

"You can't." I scrambled from the floor and rushed after her. "You'll mess up everything."

She reached for the receiver. "Mess up? If saving my granddaughter and her children from a sorry example of the human race and a life of hell is your idea of messing up, then you're not the person I'd hoped you to be. Neither of you." She pointed the receiver toward Elizabeth as she rounded the corner holding the coffee-stained blouse away from her skin.

My face burned from the verbal blow, but now wasn't the time to wallow in self-pity. Murt had already started dialing numbers. So I slapped the hook down and held it in place.

"Mamie," Elizabeth gasped. "What is wrong with you?"

"Give me a chance to talk with Lily first," I pleaded.

"Remove your hand," Murt demanded.

"If you call the police, she'll never trust me—or you—again. She'll clam up and deny everything. Is that what you want?"

Murt lifted my hand and hung up the phone. "I want that man out of their lives for good. And if that can't happen, then I want Lily and Brent here with me…safe."

"Then tell her. She needs to hear it and believe it."

"Bud and I have prayed and begged Tammy to leave Aaron Holbrook for more 'an four years, now. We've offered to go to the police with her, hire a lawyer, or do whatever it legally took to rid him from her life. He's alienated her from her friends and family, beaten her, broken her bones and her spirit. Why I'd," she looked around, yanked a large iron skillet from its peg, and swung it above her head, "bash any man's skull before he'd hurt me or my children."

I wanted to laugh at the feisty woman's display, but didn't dare. "I believe you would."

"Me, too." Elizabeth stared wide eyed, her hand covering her mouth.

Murt attempted to hide her smile as she returned the pan to its place. "I ain't never had any use for the thing, other 'an frying. My husband, Tom, was the kindest man you'd ever hope to meet."

"Listen." Elizabeth cocked her head. "It's my car. They're back," she squealed and ran for the front door with me close behind her.

The three of us stood on the front porch as two sets of headlights pulled into the driveway and stopped.

Quinn got out first and waited for Bud. I breathed a sigh when they walked up the steps, unharmed.

Bud paused in front of me. "Sorry if I worried you, Miss Mamie. But you didn't have to send Quinn after me." The corners of his mouth twitched, and then turned up. "I'd of hit Aaron, given the chance, but I wouldn't a killed him."

"You could have at least called." Elizabeth punched Quinn on his upper arm.

He winked at me. "Were you worried about me, too?"

"We was frettin' about both of you boys." Murt ushered the guys through the front door. "I'll get you all something to drink, but first, tell me about Brent. Did you get to see him?"

"I did. And it ain't good."

Murt grasped Bud's arm. "Merciful, Jesus, please don't take our boy from us."

Patting her hand, Bud helped his grandmother to the sofa. "He's goin' make it. The nurse says it'll take a while, and they're watching him real close."

"And Tammy?"

"She's scared. The police took Aaron down to the station. Seems the emergency-room doctor didn't buy the falling-down-the-stairs excuse Aaron and Tammy gave him."

"Hot-dig." Murt smiled up at all of us. "Maybe our prayers have been answered. Once he's locked away, I hope they forget where they put the key."

"Gran." Bud sat next to Murt. "Before you get too excited, I need to tell you. The social lady told me Tammy could wind up losing Brent and Lily. She mentioned a foster home."

"No!" I wanted Lily and Brent to be safe, but placing them with strangers?

Quinn slipped his hand into mine and gave it a gentle squeeze.

"They better be ready for a fight." Murt's raspy voice rose an octave. "Tammy and the kids'll stay right here."

"The social lady and Tammy know we've got Lily. And I let 'em know we ain't givin' her up. Brent, either, when he gets out of the hospital. But Tammy's a different story. She ain't in jail, but she ain't exactly in the clear, either. The police have got their eye on her."

Lily ran past me and up to Bud. "Mama's going to jail? Because of me?" She looked straight into my eyes, not waiting for Bud to answer. "You promised. You promised!"

Chapter 18

Red splotches marred Lily's pale face. Tears filled her eyes and overflowed their banks. "Why?" She gulped. "I thought you were my friend."

"I am." My heart sank like a stone tossed into Norfork Lake. For if somehow I couldn't convince her to open up and tell her family the truth, then I'd have to tell them—and the authorities—everything. She'd never forgive me. "You have a right to be mad. Your brother's in the hospital, and when Bud and Murt asked, I told them about Aaron. Not what he did or how. That's something they need to hear from you."

With pouty lips and her arms folded across her chest, Lily shook her head.

"Lily, things won't ever be better as long as Aaron's around. You want him to get away with what he's done to Brent...to your mother?" I took a deep breath to help calm my frustration. Not at Lily, but at all the Aarons in the world. "Or you?"

"The police took him. I heard Bud say so."

"Yes, but what about your mother?" I asked, ready to overstep any and all boundaries, desperate to get Lily to open up. "You heard Bud. The police have their eyes on her, too. You want her to go to jail for something she didn't do?"

"Mamie, don't," Murt ordered. "You're upsetting the child."

Too late. The trickle of tears flowing down Lily's face changed to rushing streams. Her sobs became spastic. She dropped her arms to her side and looked around the room as if mapping an escape route.

I'd added to her pain. I winced, and my heart tightened.

Bud knelt on one knee and held out his arms. "Come here, squirt."

Without hesitation, Lily reached for him and buried her face against his neck. "Mama would never hurt me or Brent. She loves us."

"Of course, she does." Bud pulled a bandana from his back pocket and handed it to her.

"Come on." Elizabeth tugged on Quinn's arm, and the two headed for the kitchen.

"You know your mother loves you, but how would the police know that?" I held my breath and waited for the response I hoped would come.

Lily pushed away from her uncle and whirled in my direction. After wiping her almost-scarlet face with the blue handkerchief, she glared at me. "I'll tell 'em!"

"And what will you say when they asked what happened to Brent?"

She stiffened and didn't utter a sound.

"She'll tell them the truth, won't you, sweetheart?" Murt patted the sofa and waited for Lily to snuggle beside her. "This child's got my blood in her and plenty of brains to know the difference between a real accident and an Aaron-Holbrook-made-up lie."

"But if we don't do and say what he tells us to," she hiccuped between words, "he'll—"

"He ain't goin' do nothin'." Bud's stood with his hands fisted at first then, to my relief, relaxed his fingers. "Not anymore. You'ins can live here as long as you want…you, Brent, and Tammy. We've got plenty of room, don't we, Gran?"

Murt gave Lily a tight hug. "More than enough. And if that cussed excuse of a man shows his face here." The old woman winked at me. "I'll reshape his head. Maybe knock some sense into him." She tapped the child's red nose. "Why if the ladies at the church caught wind of what all I'd do him, they'd place me at the top of their prayer list for sure."

For the first time all night, Lily laughed…really laughed. And the lighthearted moment became infectious.

"So," Murt continued, once the room grew quiet, "you all have gone along with Aaron's lies to cover up his dirty deeds. And if you don't, his punishments are severe. Do I have it straight?"

"Yes, ma'am," Lily answered. Her smile now gone.

"Yet his abuse continues, doesn't it?"

She squirmed and focused more on her hands folded in her lap than her great-gran's face. "Yes, ma'am."

"Then I'd say it was time to swap the lies for the truth and get shed of Aaron Holbrook, once and for all. People like him control others with meanness. Once the table's turned and he finds out you're not afraid anymore, he'll be the one shakin' in his drawers. And don't you worry none, me and your Uncle Bud and the police ain't about to let nothing happen to you."

"If I tell the truth, will Mama go to jail?"

"No, child."

But could Tammy be declared unfit, losing her rights as a mother? And if so, what then? After all, Murt was no spring chicken, and Bud was a child himself. I cringed at the possible outcome.

Lily stretched her makeshift nightshirt over her knees as she drew them to her chest and rocked back-and-forth. Then she blurted, "Brent didn't fall down the stairs. Aaron and Mama were fighting. Brent jumped in a chair…"

Pure relief bubbled up inside of me as Lily repeated the story she'd told me earlier. No doubt, Aaron had misjudged this eight-year-old.

She shared other incidences. Acts of cruelty that made my stomach churn. I don't know how many similar stories the child held inside of her. All I knew was I'd heard enough and slipped out of the room to joined Elizabeth and Quinn in the kitchen.

The two of them sat at the table. Quinn lowered his chair's front legs to the floor. "Are you okay?"

I opened cabinets, found a glass, and filled it with tap water, stalling, sipping the cool wetness until my emotions could be harnessed and tucked away. "Why wouldn't I be? Lily told Murt and Bud everything, and she's where she belongs."

"Nice try." Elizabeth sidled next to me. "You're exhausted and worried sick about that little girl in there," she waved toward the living room, "and her brother."

"I'm worried about you," Quinn chimed in. "Bud tells me, the Aaron fellow is 'one bad dude'. He also told me about the run-in you had with him. Things could get ugly if he finds out about tonight."

"That's why she'll be staying with me for the next several days." Elizabeth linked her arms with mine. "At least, until all this mess blows over."

I had no desire to have another verbal confrontation with Aaron, if or when he got out of jail. If indeed he was even in jail. Neither did I intend on living with some bossy—though well-intentioned— friend. "Men like Aaron Holbrook are cowards who feed on fear. Murt just now said as much to Lily. And I'm not going to live my life in hiding. So thanks," I glanced at Elizabeth, "but no thanks. I'm going to stay at the cabin."

Elizabeth let go of my arm. "Try to talk some sense into her while I visit the ladies' room," she ordered Quinn before scurrying out.

Too drained to argue, I plopped down in the chair opposite him and pointed my finger at him. "Please. Don't start with me."

He smiled and held up his hands. "I didn't say a word, but…"

I rubbed my throbbing temples. "The word *please* didn't mean anything, huh?"

Quinn leaned forward and rested his arms on the table. "If you'll allow me to finish my sentence." His smile stretched into a full grin.

I'd never noticed the tiny, faded scar on the left side of his chin. Perhaps because it currently stood out against the dark stubbles he now sported. "Go ahead," I answered before finishing off the glass of water, still mesmerized by his rugged and very manly appearance.

"If Aaron says anything, as much as looks at you wrong—*anything*—you have to promise to tell me." His voice demanded an answer.

It seemed strange to have anyone other than my mother express concern for my well-being, and truth be known, I was little afraid. "All right," I conceded.

"Come on." Quinn pushed his chair back as Elizabeth strolled back to the kitchen. "Let's get you girls home."

"Lily's so mad at me." My throat tightened. "But she's safe, right?"

"Are you kidding?" Elizabeth continued without waiting for an answer, "Murt may appear to be some frail old woman without an ounce of fight left in her, but after seeing the frying-pan exhibition earlier tonight." She laughed. "Lily's safety is nothing to worry about. And as for the kid being mad, she'll get over it. You'll see."

Quinn offered his hands to help me up. For the second time tonight, I didn't protest or recoil at his touch. Drained of my senses due to lack of sleep most likely.

Bud spotted us as soon as we entered the living room. "You'ins leaving?"

"Yep." Quinn looked at his watch. "It's late, and we've intruded enough."

Bud shook Quinn's hand and said something I didn't catch,

before turning to me. "Gran and me appreciate you'ins bringing Lily to us, Miss Mamie."

"We sure do," Murt chimed in.

"You're welcome." I searched Lily's face, scrambling for something to say.

Suddenly, she wiggled her finger for me to come closer and kept at it until I stood only inches away. Her expression gave nothing away. Then she wrapped her arms around my neck and squeezed tight. I'd been forgiven.

"Don't go," she whispered in my ear.

I soaked up the child's affection. "I'll be back."

"When?"

"One day this week, for sure…after work."

"Then you'll come for supper…all of you." Murt turned. "Let me get somethin' to write on." She opened a side-table drawer, retrieved pen and paper, and wrote down her phone number. "Call me Monday, and we'll work out a time."

"We don't want to impose."

"It's no bother. I 'spect we'll be in and out of town some during the day, checking on Brent and Tammy, visiting with the authorities. But there's rarely a night that goes by when I don't cook."

I folded the paper and tucked it in my pant pocket before giving Lily another hug.

As the three of us walked into the night's air, Quinn slid his hand to the small of my back. I stiffened at first, then reminded myself of the times I'd witnessed him touch Elizabeth, Janie, and Susie in the same manner. Simply a manly habit he'd developed. Nothing more.

"You sit up front with Quinn, Mamie." Elizabeth yawned. "I'll curl up on the back."

Quinn held the front passenger door and waited for me to get in. "You're trembling. Are you cold?"

He had no idea what effect his touch had on me. How could he? I didn't understand it myself. "More tired than anything else."

He shut the door and ran around to the driver's side.

"Aren't we all," Elizabeth moaned and slammed her car door. "Hey." She pointed at the dashboard after Quinn started the car. "It's after midnight, Easter Sunday. You know, we could get cleaned up, take a short nap, and still make it to the sunrise service. What do you guys think?"

Quinn shifted the car into reverse. "Sounds good."

"Mamie?" Elizabeth rested her arms across the front seat.

I closed my eyes, determined to ignore her.

"Let me word it a different way," Elizabeth whispered in my ear. "You're going."

"No. I'm. Not."

"After everything you've put me through tonight? Yes, ma'am, you are."

I twisted around. "That's blackmail."

"Call it what you want, but you *are* going."

Chapter 19

"Ouch!"

I hobbled toward the bathroom, turned on the light, and inspected my right big toe. No blood, no discoloration, only pain throbbing from where I'd stubbed it on the iron bed. Perhaps if it was broken...I held my breath and forced it to move up, and then down. But it wouldn't have mattered if the thing had been knocked clean off. Elizabeth's parting words—"You're going if I have to dress you myself"—echoed in my ear.

I glanced in the mirror. Eyes with more streaks of red than today's sunrise could possibly display blinked back at me. Matted curls, still stiff from Elizabeth's overzealous use of hairspray, clung to my head.

Water soon splattered against the shower walls. After minor adjustments, I stood under the spray and allowed the warmth to wash over me.

A dull thud dashed the cobwebs of sleep and fantasying from my mind. I stood frozen, listening. Convinced my imagination had run amuck, or perhaps the house had groaned from years of wear, I reached for the shampoo.

Crash!

The plastic bottle slipped from my fingers as glass shattered somewhere inside the cabin. My heart pounded.

I scrambled for my robe, forced my wet arms through the terry cloth sleeves, and tied the sash in a hard knot before attempting to raise the small window above the commode. It didn't budge.

"Little girl," a man's voice whispered. Glass crunched beneath footsteps.

Oh, God, please. You've got to help me! I begged, unable to move. Unable to think.

His deep, throaty laugh jarred my senses. I whirled around and flipped the light off. Within seconds, a large silhouette filled the bedroom doorway, followed by a horrible smell. An unmistakable odor. Aaron's. But hadn't Bud said—

"There you are."

I slammed the bathroom door and fumbled in the dark for the lock.

"What's the matter? Don't feel so tough anymore?"

I returned to the window—my only hope of escape—and hammered the wooden jam with the heels of both hands.

He jiggled the knob. "Come out, come out," he sang then laughed again. "You're like all the rest...stupid. That's why I'm here. Women need a man's touch every now and then. To teach them to mind their business, to treat a man with respect. To fear, honor, and obey."

No matter how hard I tried, the window wouldn't open. No phone, no heavy objects to barricade the door, and no getaway.

Aaron tapped on the door. Over and over, he drummed. The steady cadence reminded me of a funeral march. Each beat louder.

"Aaron controlled others with fear," Murt told Lily. "The tables will turn once he finds out you are not afraid."

But I was afraid. Petrified.

"Come on now," he taunted. "Might as well get it over with. Better now than later."

"Go away." My voice trembled.

"Cain't do it."

"Brent's doctors know you're responsible for his injuries. The police know it, too." My body shook all over.

"Like me and the kid's mama told 'em, he fell. Now open up before I lose my temper! You're only making it worse on yourself."

"What about breaking and entering?"

"What about it?" he huffed.

"It's against the law, and I have no reason to lie for you."

"Yeah? When I get through, believe me, you'll have one. Wouldn't be surprised if that little red car didn't find its way back to Mississippi on its own."

"Every woman's not like Tammy." My teeth chattered, making it difficult to talk. "It takes more than fear of a beating to seal their lips. For some, they'd go through almost anything to see you behind bars."

Again, he hit the door, this time the wood splintered. It wouldn't hold much longer. The window *had* to open...or break.

I groped for the commode lid, lifted it, and slammed it against what I hoped would be the panes. Sharp shards flew against my face and hands until the opening felt clear. With one foot on the seat, the other on the open tank, I pushed on the screen, and then pulled myself up.

"Gotcha."

On instinct, I screamed and tried to drag myself back inside. How could he be both places at once?

"Thought you get away, huh?"

Red-hot pain seared through my upper right leg as he drug me through the window by my hair and slammed my face against the ground.

I choked, struggling for breath, inhaling dirt, grass...everything but air.

"You are one hard-headed—"

Every muscle in my body tensed, anticipating the first blow. What was he waiting for?

"Keep your mouth shut." He tightened his grip on my hair. His weight pressed against me.

"No!" The muffled demand barely reached my ears. I tried, but couldn't budge. *God, please, somebody help me!*

Suddenly, the pressure from his body lifted. But before I could move, a punch to my right ribcage forced air from my lungs.

"I'm not finished with you," he growled next to my face. "Another day. Another time."

Frantic for air, I drew my legs and arms under me and crawled on all fours, struggling to regain the normal ebb and flow of wind.

"Mamie!"

Elizabeth? It couldn't be. I looked around. Lights blared in my eyes, blinding me. The wretched smell of Aaron faint.

"Mamie, are you okay?" Elizabeth knelt beside me. "Who was that man? What has he done to you?"

"Where...is...he?"

"He ran into the woods. Come on." She tugged. "We've got to get out of here before he comes back."

My right leg throbbed as I shifted my weight and forced myself to stand. The taste of rusty salt ran down my throat.

"Hurry!" she ordered.

I motioned her toward the driver's side while I clutched my lower right ribs and limped to the other. Only after we were both inside and the car doors locked, did I dare breathe normal.

Elizabeth backed out of the driveway, sending rocks flying. "It was Aaron, wasn't it?"

Blood saturated the terry cloth sleeve I held to my nose. "Yes."

"Did he force himself...?"

I shuddered, repulsed by the thought, reliving the feel of his body next to mine. "No."

"We've got to get you to the hospital."

"No! Your house first, so I can get cleaned up and put on something decent, then to the police station. He's got to be stopped, Elizabeth. Before he hurts someone else."

Elizabeth parked in front of City Hall, which housed Mountain Home's police station. "You ready to do this?"

I hiked up the hemline of the dress she lent me and examined the bandage on my right thigh. A dime-sized spot of blood had already soaked through the layers of gauze. "I sure wish this thing would stop bleeding."

"You need stitches." She leaned over to take a look. "But with all the bruises beginning to show on your face, a little blood to go along with the scraps and cuts on your arms and legs, maybe they'll realize they never should've let the lunatic go in the first place."

A truck roared into the parking space beside us. A black truck. Quinn's.

"What's he doing here?" I snatched the dress, covering my exposed upper leg.

"I called him." Elizabeth hit the button, unlocking her car doors as he jumped out with his hair sticking up and shirttail untucked.

"Why?"

"Because you need him."

"I what!"

Elizabeth didn't elaborate. She didn't have time. Quinn opened my door and eyed Aaron's handiwork—part of it, anyway—making me self-conscious and ashamed. "With everything Bud told me, I should've seen this coming and never allowed you to stay at the cabin by yourself."

Did he really think I would have listened?

"Come on." He held his hand out and gripped my elbow with his other one. "What do you say we put the slimeball where he belongs?"

"Hey, Quinn," the lady at the front desk greeted him, and then nodded at Elizabeth as we entered through the metal doors marked City Police. "What are y'all doing here this time of morning?"

"Who's on duty, Sarah?"

"Gary's in his office."

"Good." Quinn took my hand and led me down the hall.

"Wait," the woman ordered. But Quinn kept ushering me and Elizabeth forward.

An older Andy Griffith lookalike chuckled as we entered the second door on the left. "Got your hands full there, don't you, son?" Without waiting for an answer, the guy stood and shook Quinn's hand. "Don't know that I've ever had the pleasure of having an attorney in my office so bright and early."

Attorney? Quinn was an attorney? Why didn't I know that?

"Don't tell me this pretty little thing," he nodded toward Elizabeth, "has broken the law."

Quinn didn't make small talk. Instead, he motioned for me to sit in the worn, leather, wingback chair in front of the officer's desk while he pulled up two more for himself and Elizabeth. "I'm here with my client, Mamie Carlson—"

Client?

"—to file a complaint and make sure charges are brought against one Aaron Holbrook for breaking and entering and aggravated assault and battery for starters."

"Aaron Holbrook?" The officer sat back down and began clicking the head of the red ballpoint pen in his left hand.

"That's right. I'm sure you're familiar with him since you or one of your men recently questioned him regarding an allegation of child abuse."

"Yep." He leaned back in his chair. "Questioned him myself. Didn't believe a word he said, but with the child's mother collaborating Mr. Holbrook's story…" He shut up, as if he realized he'd already said too much, and eyed me. "From the looks of you, I assume you're the victim?"

"Yes," I answered, my head still swirling in disbelief—Quinn had been a lawyer all this time, and I never knew. Never asked what he did for a living.

"And just how do you fit into all of this?" the officer asked Elizabeth while folding over several pages of the yellow tablet before he began writing.

Elizabeth explained everything. In fact, the officer spent the better part of an hour asking the two of us questions, listening, and taking notes. I never knew it took so long to file a complaint, and I wondered why they wasted precious time when clearly someone needed to be out looking and arresting the guilty jerk.

The officer finally laid his pen down and addressed Quinn. "I guess that does it. At least, for now."

"But aren't you going to arrest him?" I asked, more than a little angry and confused by the whole process. "Look what he did to me." I pointed to my face. "Not to mention what he did to that poor child."

Elizabeth placed a hand on my arm, probably to calm me down.

Suddenly, I felt like I been hoodwinked and now, even more so, understood why most abuse victims didn't bother to file the second and third complaint.

"We'll be sending someone out to take pictures, and yes, I assure you, Mr. Holbrook will be brought in for questioning."

"Questioning!" I bolted out of my chair, too angry to care about the pain it caused. "Again? Is that all you people know how to do?"

"All part of the process, Mamie," Quinn spoke up. "But don't worry. There's more than enough evidence to support your charges and get Holbrook in front of a judge and behind bars. I promise."

"How can you…any of you," I glared all three of them, "promise me anything? And what's going to happen to Brent and Lily and their mother? Do any of you care?"

Not waiting for an answer, I whirled around and stomped out of his office and back to Elizabeth's car. "No wonder people take matters into their own hands," I muttered and doubled up my fist wanting to hit something or someone.

Elizabeth caught up with me. "I know you're angry."

"Angry? You have no idea."

"Quinn's still inside talking to Gary. He's a good lawyer, Mamie. It's in his blood. His father's one of the best. Believe me when I tell you Aaron Holbrook won't get away with what he's done to you."

"Look at me! Look at poor Brent, Lily, Tammy. Even Murt and Bud. In case you haven't been paying attention, he already has. No wonder women like Tammy never press charges. By the time the law gets off their backsides, the man has beaten the fool out of her again, and she has no choice but to drop all charges."

Chapter 20

Still fuming over the legal system's lack of gumption, I watched the doctor stick the long needle inside the three-inch gash on my right thigh.

"Try not to look."

But wanting to feel something other than the rage festering inside of me, I ignored Elizabeth and welcomed the burning sting.

He shoved the needle deeper, sideways, and then removed it only to find a new spot and repeat the process.

"Almost done." He dabbed the blood oozing from the wound. "It should be nice and numb about now."

If only they had medication to deaden my almost-uncontrollable desire for revenge.

"Now, if we can get you to lie back," the nurse lifted my legs and pulled out the lower section of the exam table, "Doc'll get you all stitched up."

The doctor, much younger than I'd expected, had already examined all my scrapes and bruises. Asked all the pertinent questions, and to my disappointment, remained expressionless when I mentioned Aaron Holbrook's name as the culprit who'd caused my injuries.

"It must get old repairing the damage from another man's brutal handiwork. Especially, when the savage's victim is an innocent child like the little boy, Brent Cunningham, who was brought in here last night. Perhaps you were the doctor on duty. The one who suspected abuse and called the police...for all the good it did."

Elizabeth squeezed my hand. Hard. But I wasn't through.

"You see, they questioned him and then let him go. So guess what...I became his next victim and your next patient. And the worst part, unless someone does something, is I won't be his last. Or yours."

The nurse glanced at the doctor, who again remained silent, his hands busy stitching me back together. I stared at the ceiling, counted the tiles, and fought the desire to scream until someone explained why the whole world had gone mad and someone like Aaron Holbrook had gone free.

"All done," the doctor finally announced. "You'll need to have your family physician take the sutures out in ten days."

Before I could announce I didn't have a doctor, Elizabeth spoke up, "Doctor McMillian will take care of it."

Great. Another bill to go along with whatever the hospital charged. Plus legal fees, the cost to repair the damages to the cabin— not to mention what I'd already spent on a new tire. After today, I'd have to eat peanut butter and jelly sandwiches for life.

"You're *not* going to do it." The early-morning sun, much like Elizabeth's temper, glared in my face as we exited the hospital. "You're not a cat, so don't push your luck."

"I've got to go back. My purse, my car...everything I own is there."

"Then make a list. I'm sure Quinn will be more than happy to get your car and any clothing you'll need."

"Allow a guy to go through my underwear and other personables?

Absolutely not. It's bad enough Quinn took the cops over to ransack the place and take pictures. If they did."

She laughed. "Quinn has sisters and a mother. It's not like he has never seen women's panties before."

"Not mine, he hasn't, and he's not going to."

She gave me a quick glance. "We're not going over there, and that's final. For all we know, this Holbrook person could still be lurking around. If it'll make you happy, we'll have one of the guys go with us this afternoon, but for now, we're headed to my place."

How could I make her understand? "It's not that I don't appreciate what you've done. I mean…if you hadn't shown up when you did… But can't you see? It won't work. Sooner or later, I'll have to decide to either leave Mountain Home, which is what Aaron hopes and expects me to do, or face him and whatever comes."

"Like you faced him this morning? In case you've forgotten." She looked around and lowered her voice. "Aaron broke into your place and dragged you out a window. God only knows what he'll do the next time."

A shudder racked me. "He caught me off guard."

Elizabeth pulled her keys from her purse. "And if he'd knocked on the front door, announced his intentions, and gave you a five-minute head start, what would you have done different, huh?"

"Maybe I should buy me a heavy-duty baseball bat."

"Funny." She wove her arm around my elbow. "Like it or not, you're moving in with me."

"What happens when Aaron finds out where I'm staying? After all, Mountain Home's not that big. It'll be a matter of time before he comes calling in the middle of the night. What then?"

"At least, I have a phone. We can call for help, and the police can come arrest him."

Aaron's words "another time, another place" were more than empty threats; they were a promise.

My right temple throbbed. "No one can keep a constant watch over me."

"God can. He kept you from Aaron's full wrath, didn't He?"

She had no idea the emotions her question stirred. Almost the instant I called out to Him, Elizabeth drove up, scaring Aaron away. Why? After I'd turned my back on Him. After not answering my prayers to heal my mama, why now?

"So we'll keep praying and trusting," she rattled on, "and let the police to their job."

"*Right.* If only they'd done their job, I wouldn't be sporting multiple stitches and a crop of bruises, would I?"

Neither of us spoke again until after we arrived at her house. "I'll find you something a little more comfortable to put on and change clothes myself." She checked her watch, then showed me the room I was to sleep in. "Mom and Dad must be wondering why I didn't show up for the sunrise service, and I know they'll be concerned when I'm a no-show for our main service."

"Why don't you go?"

"And leave you here by yourself? Not a chance. Besides, Easter is only one day out of three hundred and sixty-five we Christians celebrate what Christ has done for us. As my grandfather always says, 'Worshiping Christ is not to be confused with new clothes, colored eggs, chocolate bunnies, or a fat man in a red suit come Christmas.' How about something to eat?"

Elizabeth could change directions on me faster than a cat chasing a mouse. In my mental state, I had to rewind and hit play before able to answer, "Maybe later."

My body tensed at the room's damp coolness. I tossed the covers back, prepared to close my bedroom window. Pain and stiffness, along with the light from the hallway, reminded me where I was and why.

Clumps of Kleenex lay scattered on the nightstand and the floor. Almost half a box. My head felt as if the other half had been stuffed up my nose. Surely, Elizabeth had aspirin, Tylenol, something to help.

"Elizabeth?" I tapped lightly on the closed bathroom door. "Are you in there?"

"Mamie?"

The door flew open. "Is everything all right?" Quinn stood in front me, bare-chested. Shaving cream smeared across his face.

"I'm sorry. I thought you were—"

"It's okay." He grabbed a towel from the rack and wiped off the white foam. "I'll step out, so you…I can finish this later."

"Wait. What are you doing here? What time is it?"

"Somewhere between five and five thirty."

"Wow. It's that late?" I stifled a yawn. "Good thing I got up. A few more hours, and I would've slept the day away."

He smiled. "You did already. It's between five and five thirty *a.m.*, not p.m."

"You spent the night here?"

"On the couch."

"Why?"

"Mamie, there's no way I'm going to allow you and Elizabeth to stay here by yourselves."

What would the neighbors think seeing Quinn's truck parked in the driveway all night? And Elizabeth's parents? "Oh." I closed my eyes as the vise-grip inside my head tightened another notch. And what about the guys at work when I showed up looking like I'd been in a brawl?

"Are you okay?" He touched my arm. "Should I get Elizabeth?"

"No." My eyelids flew open.

He had dropped the towel. Swirls of black hair covered his tanned chest. I quickly tried to focus only on his face, but my peripheral vision was simply too good. "I should…" I sputtered and turned away. "I'll be out in a minute."

"Take your time. I'll scout out the kitchen and start breakfast… and don't say you're not hungry. Elizabeth said you didn't eat a thing yesterday."

"I'm really not hungry." My stomach rumbled in protest.

"You will be." He closed the door behind him.

What was it about this guy? He's my self-appointed lawyer, guardian angel, and now breakfast?

"Don't go there, Mamie," I warned myself. My body ached all over. I couldn't afford, nor was I willing, to add my heart to the list of pains.

When I walked into the hallway, there, on the floor next to my room, rested my suitcase. My face burned hot at the thought of Quinn packing my personal items.

"Hope everything's there." He handed me a glass of orange juice before reaching for the bag. "I'll set it inside your bedroom if you'd like. Then if you're ready? The eggs won't stay hot long."

In the kitchen, Quinn and I sat at the small round, glass-top table. The smell of cooked onions made my mouth water. Strings of cheese followed the bite of omelet I lifted from the plate. Diced tomatoes, along with bits of chives and red peppers, lay in folds of yellow awaiting my next taste.

Elizabeth breezed into the kitchen, all giddy and peppy. "Good morning, good morning," she sang and poured herself a cup of coffee. "How's the rib pain, Mamie?"

"Better…Maybe."

She flounced over to the table. "How's the fac—? Ooh!" Her

eyebrows shot up. "You should've allowed me to call Mr. Aldridge last night. It always goes over better when your employer's given plenty of notice. Might as well let him know you'll be out for three of four days, at least. Maybe by then, we'll be able to cover most of the discoloration with makeup."

"And maybe we won't." I pushed the plate of eggs away. "Why should I hide behind closed doors and thick makeup—I'm not the guilty party?"

"No one said you were, missy. I just don't want you scaring off Mr. Aldridge's customer—"

My heart almost jumped out of my chest at the phone's shrill next to my head.

"I'll get it." Elizabeth leaned over and picked it up, stretching the cord across the table. "Hello…. No, you didn't wake me…." She glanced my way. "Yes, she's here. Would you like?—"

I reached for the phone in hopes the police finally had gotten off their backsides and arrested Aaron, only Elizabeth pulled away, refusing to relinquish the receiver.

She covered her mouth, only partially removing it when she spoke. "Oh, Bud, I'm so sorry…. Yes, I'll tell her. Be sure and let Murt know we'll be praying…."

Praying? If prayers were needed, then Bud's call had nothing to do with the police. It was about Brent or Lilly, and it wasn't good.

Chapter 21

"Can he live without his spleen?" I paced the floor, wringing my hands. "I mean, what does it do? What's its purpose? Is it like an appendix that can be cut out and thrown away and it's no big deal?"

Quinn shrugged. "Obviously, but then medicine's not my forte."

I stopped in front of Elizabeth. "Tell me again what Bud said."

She paused as if recalling the conversation. "That his spleen ruptured, the doctors removed it during the night, and Brent's in Intensive Care."

A light came on in my head. "Wait a minute, how did he get your number, and what made him think I would be here?"

"Me." Quinn raised his hand. "I called and talked to Murt early yesterday. Gave her this number. Explained what had happened to you, and that you'd be staying here for a while. Advised them to be extra cautious. Also, for Lily's sake, suggested she come up with some kind of excuse why you wouldn't be coming for supper any time this week."

"Good idea." The last thing Lily needed to see was more evidence of Aaron's brutality. She'd never open up. "Did Murt say anything about Brent when you called?"

"No. Bud had left for the hospital, and she stayed home with Lily. Undoubtedly, Brent's condition hadn't changed, or if it had—"

"Lily will be devastated if something happens to Brent." Elizabeth plopped down at the kitchen table. "We all will, and I've never met the child."

"Will you stop it," Quinn ordered. "You've got him on his deathbed when two seconds ago Mamie wondered if removing someone's spleen was much like removing an appendix. We don't have the facts. I'm used to dealing with facts." He clipped the last two words. "So I'll run home and dress, go by the hospital, and see what I can find out, then come back and explain everything."

"They're not going to tell you squat." My disgust with the medical world and their rules spewed out much harsher than I intended. "I spent the last four years in the hospital. Trust me."

"What?" Elizabeth interrupted.

"Later." I waved her off and faced Quinn. "You're not family, *and* he's in ICU. They'll never let you back there."

"No, but they will Bud, and he can give, or get, the answers to all our questions."

"I probably won't be here." Elizabeth stared into her empty coffee mug. "There's a teacher's meeting first thing, but I'll call home later today and see what Quinn found out, Mamie."

"I won't be here, either."

The two of them stared at me as if I'd lost my marbles.

"It won't take but a minute for me to get ready. I'll follow Quinn to the hospital and, from there, leave for work."

"You can't be serious," Elizabeth huffed. "Have you bothered to look in a mirror?"

"I'm very much aware of what I look like, but hiding away is for the guilty, not the innocent." Before turning to leave the room, I eyed Quinn. "Just give me five minutes."

"Ten." Elizabeth insisted. "As much as I'm against you going anywhere, it'll take me at least that long to try to camouflage those bruises with makeup."

"Can I help you?"

Quinn and I spun toward the authoritative voice. Unable to hold eye contact as the petite brunette nurse studied my face, my gaze fell to her nametag, Sharon Smitz, RN.

"Yes, we're here to check on Brent Cunningham." Quinn spoke with equal authority, yet softer. "A patient in ICU."

"Are you family?"

"Friends."

"Then I'm afraid it's not possible."

He couldn't say I hadn't warned him.

"Even if it were, now's really not a good time. Visiting hours aren't until nine."

"Well, to tell you the truth…" Quinn reached into his pocket, pulled out a card, and handed it to the nurse. The same type card, green with gold print, he'd given me weeks earlier with Janie's address scribbled on the back. Yet I'd never bothered to read the gold print. "I'm an attorney with Ragland and Ragland, attorneys at law."

The nurse ignored Quinn and focused on a clamor down the hallway.

An elderly gentleman clung to a stretcher bedrail as two women dressed in blue scrubs rolled it from one of the rooms. "You're going to be fine, sweetheart," the gray-haired man kept repeating. Then he looked up at one of the women and asked, "Why won't she open her eyes? Why won't she talk to me? What's wrong with her?"

"Excuse me." The RN hurried toward the confusion.

My heart sank, weighted with memories as I silently prayed for the dear man whose frantic pleas echoed in the hall…and his loved one.

Then, without warning, an image of Mom's dark-blue eyes—always so full of kindness—changed into lifeless, glazed-over vacant windows.

I clutched my throat, my lungs begging for air. "I can't do this."

"Mamie?" Quinn's voiced sounded miles away.

His arms wrapped around my waist, holding me in place until the spinning stopped and the light returned.

"Elizabeth's right, you shouldn't have come." I heard him say.

My legs felt like rubber as I pulled from his grip. "The smells and the heat just got to me, that's all. I'm fine. Really."

His eyes studied mine. "No, you're not."

It took some fast-talking to convince Quinn to head to the unit without me before Nurse Smitz realized we'd taken advantage of her absence, but minutes later, I stood in front of the elevator punching the down button, still tormented by the vision. "Come on, come on."

Quinn promised he'd let me know what he found out.

I refused to promise him I wouldn't go to work.

"Wit-whew," Jim whistled as soon as I walked through the back door.

I lowered my head, trying to ignore him, and scuffed toward the back room.

"Keep your mind on your work," Dave ordered Jim. "We've got some big orders to fill."

What made me think I could pull this day off?

With one of the larger aprons tied loosely, I eyed the two tubs of ground beef at Jim's station and heaved the closest one off the counter. My ribs wouldn't allow me to forget Aaron's parting punch or hang on to the weight. The tub slipped from my hands and landed with a thud on the metal cabinet.

"You all right?" Jim asked.

I doubled over holding my side. "Not really."

147

"Why don't you take a cigarette break, Jim?"

The younger butcher chuckled. "You know I don't smoke."

"Take one anyway."

"But what about all those orders we have to fill?"

"Right. You stay here and start wrapping. And listen for any customers at the deli. If Mr. Aldridge needs me, tell him I'll catch up with him later." Dave wiped his hands against his apron, looked at me, and nodded toward the back door. "Outside."

Once we stepped out on the dock, I didn't wait for Dave to start in on me. "Whatever you have to say, just say it and get it over with."

"All right." His eyes locked on mine. "What's going on? And don't tell me nothing. I'd rather be told to shut up and mind my own business than to be lied to."

"I'm not feeling well."

He leaned forward, squinting. "I can *see* that. You been in a car wreck, Mamie, or is there some other explanation for…?" He waved his hand toward my face.

"A friend did my makeup this morning. She got a little heavy handed."

"Um-hm. Well, I don't know much about makeup, but I've had my share of black eyes growing up. Looks like someone got 'heavy handed' with more than makeup. You go out drinking, partying, and scrapping on your off time, it's one thing, but when it interferes with work, it's another. Understand?"

Too distraught to handle another emotion upheaval, I nodded and let him think what he wanted to.

"Good." He backed away. "But you don't hit me as that type of girl. What's his name?"

"What?"

"The loser boyfriend who hit you. And I'm guessing he punched you in the ribs. Am I right?"

My bottom lip quivered. "About the ribs, but not about the boyfriend."

"You want to tell me about it?"

I blinked away the tears. "A man broke into my place yesterday. I tried to get away, but…"

"Did you know this guy?"

"Vaguely." I wrapped the massive apron's excess ties around my finger. "I stopped him from smacking an innocent little boy. Seems he took offense. My friend came to pick me up for a sunrise service. She scared him off, or it might have been worse."

Dave clenched his fingers into a fist. "Does this fellow have a name?"

"Aaron Holbrook."

"Never heard of him, but I expect the police have. You did press charges, right?"

"Yes." *For all the good it did.* "But unless they've arrested him in the last hour, he's still out there."

"No man *ever* has the right to mistreat a woman and child. If you were my daughter, he'd know that, and the police wouldn't have to worry about arresting him."

But I wasn't his daughter. I was only an employee. "I want to work. I *need* to work."

"And I'd rather you didn't."

"Please," I begged. "If I go home, I'll be there by myself, tuned in to every sound. Reliving every detail."

His eyebrows all but met at the bridge of his nose as he studied my face once again. "No picking up anything heavy. Two—not one—*two* fifteen-minute breaks and a full thirty-minute lunch break. Jim will work the deli. I don't want the customers bombarding you with nosy questions you have no obligation to answer, and I'll be keeping an eye on you. If I think you need to go home, you go home. Understand?"

"I promise."

"If you need a place to stay, my wife and I—"

"Thanks," I answered, stunned by his offer. "But I'm staying with a friend."

"Good." He reached to open the door. "One more thing before we go inside. Until the guy's behind bars, you don't leave without either Jim or me escorting you to your car."

I nodded, again amazed by this man who'd turned out so different from what I'd judged him to be the first day we met.

Chapter 22

After nine, and still no word from Quinn. How long did it take to ask a few questions and drive a few miles or pick up a phone?

"Good morning, Mrs. French. What can I get for you, today?"

I cringed at Jim's greetings. Here I stood, silently chastising Quinn when I'd yet to notify the woman I rented from about the damage to her cabin.

"Where's Mamie? Is she sick?"

"No, ma'am, she's here. We've got her busy in back, so I'm sort of helping out."

"Seems to me it'd make better sense if you stayed in the back and she worked out here. After all, we customers like consistency."

"Normally I'd agree, but we're trying to make it a little easier for her today."

"Oh?"

Dave's knife clanked against the metal table at the same time the package of beef I'd just slapped the price sticker on slipped through my fingers and hit the floor.

"Jim," Dave barked. "I need to see you. *Now.*"

Within seconds, Jim stood in front of Dave with me straining to hear the conversation. "You don't have the sense God gave a billy goat," Dave hissed.

"What'd I do?" Jim held his hands out, glancing back-and-forth between me and Dave.

Dave leaned across the table, his jaw set firm. "You were about to let that old busybody milk every gossiping morsel right out of you. What happened to Mamie this weekend is none of her business…or anyone else's."

"Y'all know me better than that," Jim responded in his ever-present jovial style. "Besides, I don't exactly know what all *did* happen to Mamie. Nobody tells me anything."

Actually, she had every right to know. Two broken windows for sure, maybe more.

Ding, ding, ding.

"Young man, I don't have all day."

"Get out there before she has a complete hissy fit," Dave ordered Jim. "And swing the door closed on your way out. Mamie, you go take a break. The last thing I need is her spotting you back here and asking even more questions."

The bottled Coke landed with a thud as coins clanked into the machine's small change compartment. Streaks of moisture rolled down the green glass surface as frosty gases escaped with a fizz from its opened top. My mouth watered, waiting the tasty treat.

"There you are."

Dabbing my chin with the back of my hand, I spun around. "Mr. Aldridge?"

A twinge of guilt scorched my cheeks. Had he noticed how behind the market had gotten or poor Jim doing the work of two people?

"I'm so sorry. Dave told me what happened. He didn't go into a lot of details, but I could tell he was upset." Mr. Aldridge lightly touched my forehead. "I can see why." Fishing in his pocket, he produced a Snickers bar. "You like chocolate?"

"Does a pig love mud?" I laughed, hoping to make light of the awkward moment.

"I owe you an apology, Mamie. A few weeks back you asked for my advice about a woman you thought was being mistreated."

"And you gave it." I smiled, remembering his words. "You said to get my facts straight. I was working on that part. And you also said, according to most policemen, when it comes to domestic disputes, I might end up hurt. Seems you were right about that, also."

"Unfortunately." He shook his head. "It shouldn't be, but too often that's the way it works out. But I hope you realize this sort of thing doesn't normally happen in Mountain Home. We're a small community with one of the best sheriffs and finest police officers you'll ever find."

So far, I wasn't impressed, but I didn't dare dispute him. As for small communities being immune to their share of Aarons, I had my doubts there also.

"Oh, I almost forgot." He reached in his other pant pocket, pulled out a slip of paper, and handed it to me. "Quinn Ragland called. Nice guy. Know him and his dad well. Anyway, he says he'll be at this number for the next thirty minutes."

"Finally."

"One more thing, Mamie."

"Yes, sir." I stood on one foot and then the other wondering how much of the thirty minutes had already passed.

"Fanny French insists I find out why Jim's working the deli and not you. I gather she doesn't know about the break in."

"No, sir."

"News travels fast. It would be better if she heard it from you, and I suspect she'll be headed straight home when she leaves here. The milk and ice cream in her buggy won't hold up long in this heat."

"Yes, sir, right after I talk to Quinn."

"And don't overdo," he ordered before leaving.

I wasted no time dialing the number on the paper Mr. Aldridge had given me. Quinn picked up on the first ring.

"Thank goodness, you're still there."

"I've only got a minute, so we'll have to make this brief. Here's what I found out. Yes, a person can live a normal life without a spleen. Brent may be a little more prone to infection than most kids and have to stay up on his immunizations. For now, he's holding his own and will probably be in ICU for the next day or so."

"What does that mean, holding his own?"

"It means he's not going backward."

"But it means he's not going forward, either, right?"

"According to Bud, the doctors expect a full recovery. Look, I can't keep my client waiting any longer. I'll explain everything, in detail, tonight. Meanwhile, try not to worry. See you tonight."

Somewhat relieved about Brent, I tried to think of how I'd explain the damage to Mrs. French's cabin. After all, I'd not been inside since being dragged out the bathroom window. I wasn't sure myself what the place looked like. But as it did for a child sent to the bathroom in wait of a spanking, the dread would continue to mount until the story was told, so I reached for the phonebook.

"It's about time," Elizabeth scolded as she met me at the front door, dressed in her cute yellow bermuda shorts. "Look who finally decided to show up, y'all," she announced over her shoulder.

Susie fingered the gold cross dangling from the chain around her neck. "We've been so worried about you."

"We both have." Janie shocked me by hugging my neck as if we were long-lost cousins. "Bless your heart." She stepped back. "Let me take a good look at you."

In spite of Janie bragging about Elizabeth's makeup job and how the bruises were hardly noticeable, Susie's strained smile and wrinkled nose said otherwise.

Elizabeth tried to steer me toward the couch. "Quinn's out looking for you."

"Why?" I looked around for a clock. "What time is it?"

She twisted the watch around on her wrist. "After seven. He was afraid you'd had a flat, maybe stopped by the hospital."

"I had to meet Mrs. French at the cabin."

"How'd that go?"

Before I could answer Elizabeth, Susie blurted, "How could you stand to go back there? Why I would've died if someone broke into my place. Simply *died*."

The way she clutched her chest with such flare and drama and whined with true, sweet Southern charm, I almost suspected she might actually be experiencing heart palpations.

Elizabeth dropped her arm around Susie's shoulders. "Why don't we all sit down and let Mamie catch her breath. She can tell us all about her meeting with Mrs. French."

"First of all, until today, I've not gone back since the night Aaron broke in. So I think I was as shocked as Mrs. French. Quinn did a good job boarding up the two windows and cleaning up the glass, but the bathroom door… The frame was all splintered." For a second, I had a few palpations of my own, visualizing the proof the lock wouldn't have held another onslaught.

"Oh, Mamie! It's a wonder—"

Elizabeth patted Susie's hand and encouraged me to continue.

"To the right of the door, a crack in the Sheetrock traveled halfway up the wall. All I kept hearing was Mrs. French telling me

155

'you tear it up, you fix it' the day she agreed to rent me the cabin."

Janie crossed her arms and smiled. "From what I understand, Mrs. French has quite the temper and a vocabulary to go along with it."

"Janie," Elizabeth chastised.

The girl held her hands up and lowered her head. "Just repeating what I've been told."

"Well, don't." Elizabeth's take-charge attitude kicked in. A trait that sometimes tried my patience to the hub, but a trait I had begun to admire and somewhat appreciate. "Go ahead, Mamie."

"I promised to pay her back every cent it cost to repair everything, no matter how long it took. That's when she cupped my chin and told me, 'You'll insult me if you try.'"

"She plans to press charges against Aaron, have her insurance agent take a look at the damages, get a few bids, and, hopefully, have it ready for me to move back in before the end of the month."

"You will not," Elizabeth practically screamed. "What if that maniac decides to come back? No, absolutely not."

"You know I can't stay here forever, and that's how long it may be before that man's ever put behind bars."

"Oh, ye of little faith."

Susie shrieked at the unexpected sound of Quinn's voice. At the same time, I bolted off the couch ready to fight or flight until I spotted him at the front door.

His eyes pierced mine. "Where have you been?" he growled. "I've been looking everywhere."

"Sorry, but Mrs.—"

"I've a good mind to take your car keys away."

Even though he said the words with a smile, heat crawled up my neck and into my cheeks, adding shades of red that surely dimmed the layers of blush Elizabeth painted on earlier. No longer able to

156

harness my anger over the events of the past two days, I sashayed over and stood almost toe to toe with Mr. Quinn Ragland, arched my neck to make sure he received the full impact of the daggers my eyes threw, and jabbed a finger against his chest. "Who do you think you are coming in here, yelling at me, threatening to take my keys away?"

He took a step back. "I'm not threatening. I'm just concerned and trying to keep you safe. That's all."

"Well, let me tell you something, mister." I poked his chest again. Hard. So hard my knuckle cracked. "You don't own that car, and furthermore, you *don't* own me. I'll go anywhere, anytime without answering to you or any man."

Quinn raked his fingers through his hair. "Mamie, I'm sorry. I didn't mean to upset you."

I grabbed my purse and keys off the end table and headed for the front door, needing time and space to cool off. To try to analyze what it was about Quinn Ragland that riled me so stinking bad.

"Oh, no, you don't." Without warning, Quinn scooped me in arms—his square chin set firm—and headed toward Elizabeth's guest bedroom. The room I'd been staying in.

"Put me down," I ordered, squirming against his rock-hard chest. "I mean it. Put. Me. Down."

"Or what?" He shoved the door closed with his foot.

Chapter 23

"You are the most stubborn, thickhead, cantankerous woman I've ever known." Quinn lowered my feet to the floor.

"I don't think too much of you, either." I untwisted my blouse and smoothed it over my exposed midriff.

"That first night at the lake, I said it then and I'll say it again, you don't trust anyone."

"For good reasons, wouldn't you say, Mr. Attorney? Take a good look at me."

"The lack of trust I'm talking about came long before Aaron Holbrook."

"People have to earn my trust, and in case you're wondering, you haven't."

"What are you afraid of, Mamie? Who hurt you so badly that now any man who tries to pry his way into your life has to pay for someone else's wrongdoing?"

"You're crazy."

"You put up a great front. Tough girl who doesn't need or want for anything. How many years have you been working at it? Five? Ten? A lifetime?"

"What are you, a lawyer or a psychiatrist?"

"Someone who cares. A lot."

"Better not let your girlfriend find out." I smirked, hoping to turn the table. Put the spotlight on him. "Bad enough you're spending so much time over here and not enough time with her."

"Girlfriend?" He chuckled. "Is this your way of asking if I have one?"

Heat spread from my neck plum up to my ears. "Don't act stupid."

"Hey," he took a step back and held up his hands, palms out, "who's acting? I have no idea what you're talking about."

Like a light switch, his tone of mockery turned my moment of embarrassment into rage. I wanted to scream, throw him out. "Why do men always feel they have to lie?" I asked calmly, refusing to waste my energy or give him the satisfaction of knowing he'd gotten to me. "Is it part of your DNA? Something you're taught from birth?"

Quinn rubbed his chin, unsuccessfully covering the smile underneath. The one his dimple and the laugh lines outlining his deep-chocolate eyes gave away. "There *is* no girlfriend."

"So the tall, blonde girl with the white Firebird—the one I saw you kiss—means nothing, hum?"

He removed his hand, allowing a naughty grin to curl his lips upward. "Well, now that you mention it, she does sound vaguely familiar."

"If the poor girl was smart, she'd kick your behind to the curb." Part of me wanted to smack him for her.

"Now, hold on." He snagged my hand when I attempted to walk past him. "It's my turn. First of all, the person you just described is my sister."

"Sister?" No way. I snatched my hand from his. "You hugged and kissed her."

"On the cheek."

"Sorry, but it looked more than the typical nice-to-see-you-today-sis greeting. Try again."

"She drove down for a visit. We hadn't seen each other in over a year. Our family's close."

"Um-hum."

"It's true. I still kiss my mother and hug my dad, but hey, I'm flattered to know it upset you to see me with a girl."

"*Oh pllh—eeease.*" I groaned out the word and rolled my eyes for good measure. "What's it to me who or how many girls are in your stable? Here's what you *do* need to know though: You ever try to manhandle me again, and I'll claw your eyeballs clean out of your head."

He crossed his chest with his finger. "Promise. Anything else?"

"Yes." I brushed past him and opened the door. "Get out."

He turned to leave. "Okay. I guess that means you're not interested in hearing about Brent's condition or how—"

"Wait." I scooted in front of him. "How is he?"

Quinn leaned against the nearby wall, his arms crossed. "I'm not going to lie to you. Brent's one sick little boy. When the spleen ruptured, blood spilled into the abdominal cavity. That can be fatal if not caught in time, from what the doctor told Bud. However, the surgery went well. Brent's condition is listed as guarded, but barring any unforeseen problems, he'll be back pestering his big sister in no time."

I release a pent-up breath. "That's this time. What happens next? Aaron's still out there, you know?"

"Something you should be more mindful of. Turns out the coward—according to an extensive criminal record check—has made aggravated assault and battery his life's ambition. He's been fined, sentenced to community service, placed on probation, and incarcerated multiple times since the age of fourteen. Earned himself time in Juvie for assaulting his mother, but that didn't seem to slow him down any. From Texas to here, it's more of the same. Petty theft, numerous DUIs along the way. Rape charges some lawyer got him off due to technicalities. Assault and battery, many of which ended up dropped."

"Why?"

"Why do you think?"

The room suddenly grew as cold as M&H's walk-in cooler. Quinn didn't have to spell it out. Making someone else's life hell on earth only proved rehabilitation didn't work for some.

"Now, maybe you understand why I went a little crazy when you didn't call and didn't show up right after work. So no more gallivanting off without telling me or Elizabeth. Deal?"

I nodded, not trusting my voice to form the words.

"Oh, and one more thing." He leaned in close. "I know you don't trust me—or anyone else for that matter—but I intend to make sure Aaron Holbrook—nor anyone else—ever hurts you again." He pushed himself from the wall and unfolded his arms. "And that's a promise."

Moonlight trickled through a gap between the curtains, casting a band of silver across the foot of my bed. Each tick from the nightstand clock added to the two hours I'd already rolled and tossed. I threw aside the covers and switched on a nearby lamp. Its glow chased away the night shadows but not the memory of Aaron's filthy hands on me or his promising he wasn't through with me. Nor did it quell my concerns for Brent and Lily.

"Mamie?" A rap on my bedroom door followed Elizabeth's voice. "Can I come in?"

"Sure." I slipped into my robe and greeted her at the door. "What's wrong?"

"That was my question. On my way from the bathroom, I noticed your light on. Are you still worried about Aaron?"

"Yes and no."

"Brent?"

"He's crossed my mind more than once tonight."

Elizabeth sat with her back against the footboard. "I can't help but wonder why a woman picks a guy like Aaron, much less stays with him."

"I've wondered the same thing, but I'm sure most men aren't stupid enough to show their true colors right off. So, unfortunately, the poor girl doesn't figure out she has picked a cheating, conniving scumbag until after she's married. Or in Tammy's case, allowed him to move in, take over, and then refuse to leave."

Elizabeth's eyebrows jumped halfway to her hairline. "You don't think too highly of the opposite sex, do you?"

"Let's just say I don't believe most of them can be trusted."

"Neither can all women. That's why Memaw says, 'Don't fall in love with the chandelier without checking out the foundation first.'"

"What on *earth* are you talking about?"

She laughed and pulled her knees to her chest. "Memaw explained it like this, 'no matter how pretty the house may be, always check its foundation before making a lifetime commitment,' and 'never date a guy whose feet aren't firmly planted on Christ. Otherwise, you may find too many undesirable flaws that'll never hold up through the first storm.'"

"Hum." I thought of my parents. "Makes sense."

"I've always thought so. And it sure beats condemning the entire male species. Not to mention *yourself* to spinsterhood, right?"

"Probably." I raked a wisp of hair out of my eyes and wondered if it was possible ever to change my attitude toward men. After all, I'd spent the better part of my life sizing them up and cutting them down.

She slid her feet into her pink slippers. "I'll see you in the morning."

"So why haven't you found Mr. Right?"

Elizabeth's smile lit her whole face. "Who says I haven't?"

"Really?" I asked, floored. "Why haven't you said anything? Who?"

She giggled, covering her mouth to muffle the sound. "You've met him. That first night at Janie's. Remember? Christopher?"

"The accountant?"

"He came by Sunday, but you were asleep. This time of year, I don't see him much. Last-minute tax returns. It's amazing how many people wait until the last minute to file. You have filed yours, I trust?"

"Yep." Filed, got my return, and close to spending my last dime.

"Good for you. And good for me the fifteenth is only eight days away."

"So you like him a great deal, then?"

"Like him, love him, and plan on marrying him someday, but that's a conversation for another time. Try to get some sleep."

But sleep didn't come. I paced the floor with my thoughts and insides twisting like yards of knotted yarn. Aaron's wicked grin flashed before my eyes one minute. Next, I'd wrestled with the thought of leaving Mountain Home.

How did I get into this mess? How does someone like Aaron Holbrook become so evil, inflicting pain without an ounce of remorse? Then suddenly, I was reminded how I'd turned my back on God and how hard I'd seared my heart with bitterness. With time, could I grow as cold and cynical, perhaps as evil?

"God, I don't want to be angry anymore…or afraid, but I don't want to be hurt or an emotional cripple like my mother and Tammy all because of some man."

The next morning, Jim stood at his station. The meat grinder growled as he forced chunks of beef down its throat with a wooden mallet. Reflections from the overhead lights flashed against the knife while Dave deboned, with precision and speed, the quartered carcass.

Neither of them expected me this time of morning. From my first day, I'd been warned not to touch or approach Dave while he worked. So I pushed the door closed forcefully enough to draw their attention.

Almost simultaneously, the two men looked up. Jim flipped the machine off. His face spread into a wide toothy grin. "Girl, what are you doing here this time of day?"

"With all the extra breaks I took yesterday and you working the deli, we stayed so far behind. So I thought I'd come in a few minutes earlier." Plus, more now than ever, I felt so awkward and self-conscious around Quinn.

"I thought I told you to take it easy this week." The scowl on Dave's face, a look I now realized masked his kindheartedness, had lost all its intimidation.

"You did, but I can do this. I really want to."

Dave glanced at a piece of paper I knew to be today's work orders. "All right." He nodded toward tubs piled high with meat ready to wrap, weigh, and price. "But the rules still stand. You're not to pick up anything heavy, and you're to take your full breaks with extra ones when I say so."

I'd opened my mouth to protest, but Jim cleared his throat and wagged his head. I clamped it shut.

Tiny lines deepened around Dave's laser-blue eyes. The corners of his mouth turned upward, ever so slightly as he refocused on his work.

This was his market. His word was law, and I had grown to respect him.

Chapter 24

Friday, and still, the police had encountered very few leads on Aaron's whereabouts.

"There's always a chance he has skipped town," Quinn told me on more than one occasion.

The best news I'd had all week came Wednesday when Brent was moved from ICU to Pediatrics. In spite of my hang-ups with hospitals, I wanted so badly to visit the precious tow-haired little boy who'd made a forever mark on my heart. Hopefully, I'd have a chance to talk with his mother then. But not until the bruises and scrapes on my face healed. She and Brent needed to see a friendly face, not one that mirrored the handiwork they each knew all too well. For that same reason, I'd only been able to talk to Lily by phone. Her pleas to come see her broke my heart.

"We're going to be late if you don't hurry."

Elizabeth's warning pulled my attention back to the flattened curls lifeless and stuck to my head after being free from the snood and multiple bobby pins. There wasn't time for a major do-over, not after taking a long hot bath. So with dampened hands, I bent over and finger combed each section until the multiple layers of hairspray released their hold and the bounce somewhat returned.

Truth be known, I didn't feel like dinner and games at Janie's.

"It's me." Quinn's muffled voice came from somewhere in the living room, followed by the thud of the front door. "Are y'all ready to go?"

I stepped out into the hallway wearing the only decent jeans I owned, a flower-printed peplum top, and a forced smile. "Whenever y'all are."

Janie went all out. Roast, so tender a knife wasn't needed; cream potatoes with small puddles of butter on top; green beans she proudly announced she and her mother had canned last spring, and corn on the cob. But her homemade yeast rolls impressed me most. Warm. Practically melted in my mouth. This girl could cook, and the guys complimented her by having seconds and thirds and spouting more than once what a great catch she'd make some lucky man. I just hoped if she ever decided to marry, the guy would value her for more than her beauty and culinary abilities.

After supper, we girls loaded the dishwasher and put everything away while Travis and Quinn set up the Monopoly board. So we thought. Instead, we found them in the living room rubbing their stomachs.

"Quinn and I've decided we should do something a little more active, like charades, to work off the groceries we just packed away."

"That's right," Quinn added. "And tonight, instead of it being dames against gents—since we're always outnumbered these days with Christopher slaving away—why don't we partner up? Have three teams?"

"I've got Janie," Travis shouted.

"Then I pick the newbie." Quinn looked my way and winked.

Elizabeth threaded her arm through Susie's. "Fine with us. Bring it on."

Every one of them took winning serious, much more so than the first time they introduced me to the game. Made me feel like a chicken in a swimming contest with a family of ducks. But Quinn refused to let me drown. Instead, he had me laughing. And there were no snarky remarks, unlike Travis, when time ran out before I guessed the correct answer or left my partner clueless with my antics.

Before the game ended, Janie insisted we break for root-beer floats.

"Sounds good to me." Travis fell back on the sofa and propped his feet on the glass-topped coffee table. "As Elizabeth said earlier, 'bring it on'."

"Mamie, do you mind giving me a hand?"

"I will," Susie volunteered.

"That's okay," Janie insisted. "The two of us can handle it. Right, Mamie?"

"Sure." Shocked but pleased she'd asked, I pulled my legs under me and pushed off from the brown beanbag chair. From the overstuffed tan sofa, to the slender chrome floor lamp, Janie's living room mirrored a page right out of *Better Housekeeping*.

In the kitchen, Janie's smile and peppy persona dissipated. "You dip." She handed me the metal scoop and set the frosty mugs and a tub of ice cream in front of me. "I'll fix Susie's. She's diabetic, you know?"

How could I forget? "Yes, I remember."

"There's something I have to know." She reached over me for one of the foggy mugs. "Is it true, you moved here without a stick of furniture to your name?"

I jammed the scoop into the frozen dessert, not because of the question, but her sarcastic tone. "That's correct."

"Who does that?" She lifted her chin. Or was it her nose? Whichever, she looked down at me like an old woman trying to see through her bifocals. "I mean—just curious, mind you— but I'd have to be running from someone, or *something,* to leave everything I owned behind. Travis thinks it could be someone. In lieu of what's happened to you, perhaps he's right. Should we be concerned? After all," she busied herself dipping from the small container of sugar-free ice cream, "we hardly know you."

My fingers itched to shove her face inside the bucket in front of me.

"What's taking y'all so long?" Quinn stood in the doorway. "Not my words, Travis's."

Janie's smile and laughter suddenly returned. "Oh, you know how we girls are." She pranced over and slipped her arm through the curve of his. "Talk, talk, talk. And the more we talk, the slower we get. But now that you're here, would you be a doll and loosen the caps on these two sodas? I'm afraid I've got the grip of a kitten."

And the fangs and claws of a wildcat. I wanted to add.

"No problem." A pressurized hiss followed the snap of each cap. Quinn then began pouring the fizzy drink into the glasses I'd filled.

"Whoa." I grabbed a paper towel, ready to clean the brown foam rising high and spilling over a few rims.

"Don't worry." He waved me off. "I've got this. You just finish filling that last mug, and we're out of here."

"I've decided to skip dessert." What I really wanted was to skip out on the rest of the evening.

"Nonsense."

"No, really," I insisted. "I'm not real fond of root beer."

His smiled widened. "Janie, got any Hershey syrup, cocoa, Oreo cookies? Anything chocolate?"

"There's syrup in the fridge. Why?"

He didn't bother to answer or pay any attention to my protests. Instead, he soon concocted the biggest sundae I'd ever seen. Even topped it with other findings from the refrigerator, whipped cream and a Maraschino cherry.

He wiped his hands on a drying cloth and draped it over his right shoulder. "Voila!" He presented his masterpiece. "May not top S'mores, but you can't say I didn't try."

"I can't eat all that."

"Good." He took the spoon and helped himself to a humongous bite. "We'll share."

"What am I supposed to do with the extra float?" Janie whined.

"Travis," he answered around a mouthful of sundae before refilling his spoon and aiming it toward my mouth.

With pouty lips, Janie folded her arms across her chest. "Could you two at least help me get everyone *else* served?"

Mischief lit Quinn's eyes. "No problem." Then he twisted his head toward the doorway and sang out, "Come and get it."

Janie's lips tightened. Quinn drizzled more chocolate on our dessert, oblivious to the dagger-filled glare Janie aimed my direction.

"I hear they've been tearing the bass up this week," Travis announced as he entered the kitchen. "What do you say, Quinn, if it's nice tomorrow morning, you want to take the boat out? Get some fishing in? That is if you're not tied up guarding the henhouse."

"Not this hen." Elizabeth laughed. "I promised Christopher I'd help crunch numbers and file papers."

"Me, either." I took another bite of mostly chocolate, in hopes of dousing the taste of bitter regret over not being able to try my hand at the sport Doris praised so.

Janie's eyes fluttered; her smile returned. "Then I say, let's do it, Travis. You, Susie, me, and Quinn." She glanced my way. "The four of us. Just like old times."

Was that it? Jealousy? Of me?

The thought both amused and saddened me. What kind of threat could she possibly see in me?

The next morning, I woke to Quinn humming and water splattering against the tub floor and walls. I scooted toward the kitchen, convinced I'd have enough time to get breakfast started before he finished his shower and shave.

Soon the coffee's burnt, bitter aroma overpowered the sweet mixture of cinnamon, sugar, and butter waiting to be spooned out on the flat layer of raw dough.

"What are you up to?" Elizabeth yawned and slid her slippered feet against the tile floor, approaching a nearby cupboard to retrieve her favorite white mug with Canada printed under the single maple leaf. A souvenir from one of her many trips as a child with Memaw and Papa.

"Cinnamon biscuits. Mom used to make 'em, or either chocolate gravy to go on her plain biscuits, every Saturday when I was little."

"Chocolate gravy?" She curled up her lip. "Yuck. We may have to take a vote before you spring that dish on us."

"Very funny." I finished slicing the rolled log of dough and began placing them on the lightly buttered cookie sheet. I would wait and tell her after breakfast, but after today, she'd have her kitchen back. And her privacy. For Mrs. Fanny had called me at work yesterday to let me know the guys had completed their work at the cabin.

Chapter 25

A shard of glass winked at me from the orange carpet fibers. A calling card. A reminder. As if I needed one.

The heavy iron/glass security door banged shut behind me. It, along with paneled windows throughout, had been installed for my safety according to Mrs. French. So why didn't I feel safe?

My stomach fluttered. My hands shook as I forced my way to the bedroom. Plaster, a new wooden door, and the toxic smell of fresh paint could never erase the memory of Aaron's madness and determination to inflict pain…or worse. What were his full intentions? Thoughts tormented me night and day. What was he capable of? And the big question, why couldn't the police find him?

I tossed my suitcase on the bed then hurried back into the kitchen to unload my small grocery purchases for the week. The stench of soured milk oozed from the refrigerator as soon as I opened it, attacking my nose and burning my eyes. I gagged as I poured the clabbered liquid down the drain and rinsed out the carton, but the odor, refusing to be washed away, permeated every square inch of the little cabin. Another reminder of *that* night. Opening windows to air out the place wasn't an option. Waving fabric sheets around the room proved to be a waste of time.

Giving up, I turned on the TV and plopped on the couch, staring at more snowy static than picture. Hissing and crackling even drowned out the voices. A problem going outside and manually repositioning the antenna may or may not have been remedied.

A prisoner. That's what I'd become. Unable to live free of fear. Unable to come and go without being constantly aware of my surroundings. Not daring to go out at night without someone with me. Even Dave and Jim still wouldn't allow me to walk to my car alone after work. And sleep? Would a full night's sleep, free of Aaron's haunting words and evil face, ever be a pleasant reality again?

A chill ran through me. The reality enough to make me pack up and move on. The thought, brewing for days, always left a bitter taste. Why should I allow a man's actions to dictate where and how I lived? Otherwise, I'd never find my spot in the world. Besides, since moving to Mountain Home, I'd discovered not all men were jerks. Even Dave, given the chance, proved to be nothing more than a grumbly teddy bear. Jim a delight to work with. Mr. Aldridge always more than fair. And Quinn…

Without warning, this morning's vision of Quinn standing in the living room, buttoning his shirt, painted itself in my mind. Exposed black hair against a well-developed, tanned chest caught my eye. Again. Only this time, I'd not looked away. Instead, I remembered Memaw's words of wisdom Elizabeth had shared with me regarding finding the right man.

"He makes one fine-looking chandelier, Memaw." Bronze, glowing manners, bright smile. Most girls would love to have him as a permanent fixture in their life.

A car door slamming erased thoughts of Quinn.

I sprang from the couch and flipped off all the lights. The glow from outside, the one outlining the curtains, vanished as well.

With arms out straight, I swept the air in front of me. In the bedroom, my fingers frantically searched for the scissors atop the chest. I gripped the cold metal handles in my fist, the points out, ready to strike. In the living room, I positioned myself between the door and front window. Running had proven not to be an option.

"God, if I have to, please give me the mental and physical strength."

Eeerk.

A porch board protested.

My eyes tried to bat the blackness away. My heart pounded, the rush of blood heightening all my senses.

"Mamie."

Elizabeth?

I gulped in air and slapped the lights on before swinging the door open wide. I wanted to hug her neck, thank her for coming, but then she'd know how afraid I really was. "What are you doing here?"

"Movin' in." She stepped inside with a suitcase.

I let out a fake laugh. "You're kidding."

"Do I look like I'm kidding?" She held the luggage in front of my face and then gripped her nose. "What is that smell?"

"But I've only got the twin bed you gave me."

"Fine. I'll sleep on the couch."

"You can't."

"Okay, you take the couch; I'll sleep in the bed. Doesn't matter to me." She headed for the bedroom. "But we've got to air this place out."

I moved between her and the doorway. "Why are you doing this?"

"Because you're too stubborn to stay at my place and let Quinn watch after us. Because I care. Because," she eyed the scissors in my hand, "you're scared to death and you know it."

She had me dead out. "And you aren't?"

"Look, I'm not too proud to admit it. I'd much rather be sleeping at my place than at the scene of the crime. With no telephone, I might add."

"Even if Quinn has to sleep on your couch for the next six weeks?"

"You don't hear him complaining, do you? But if it's his comfort you're worried about, we *could* all stay at his grandmother's where there'll be more than enough room."

"Right." I rolled my eyes, not caring if she noticed. "Like Granny wouldn't mind."

"Mrs. Randall died last winter. But no, she wouldn't. She was one of the sweetest people I've ever met. That, and she thought the world of Quinn."

"*Three's Company* makes a good sitcom, but I wouldn't think Quinn's family would take too kindly—or think it a bit funny—if all of us pile into the family homestead. Besides, what about Quinn? Don't you think he should have a say in all of this?"

"It was his idea. But hey," she shrugged, "don't take my word for it. Ask him yourself. He's sitting out there in his truck. Guarding the house. Where he'll be sleeping for the next, who knows how long, because someone we know won't cooperate."

I moaned and rolled my eyes again. "He is not."

Like a dog with a bone, not willing to give it up, Elizabeth marched to the front window and yanked the curtain back. "Take a look."

Only the parking lights suggested a black truck set out there engulfed in the now-thick cover of night.

I stepped back, embarrassed, knowing he could clearly see us gawking at him. "This is crazy."

She dropped the curtain, along with her suitcase, and spun my direction. "You're right. So why don't you go pack your things so we can get out of here?"

I didn't bother to tell her I never unpacked.

"Come on, Mamie. Be reasonable."

Earlier today, I thought I was being reasonable, but now…

"Okay." I raised my hands, surrendering to reality. I might not be able to stay here by myself ever again—thanks to Aaron Holbrook. "I give up." For now.

Elizabeth rode with me. I followed Quinn.

"How much farther?" I backed off the gas pedal, tired of choking on the dust Quinn's truck kicked up.

"Not far."

"That's what you said fifteen minutes ago."

Elizabeth twisted around and looked in the back. "I'd hate to have a wreck in this thing. It's not much bigger than a go-cart."

"Wonder why Quinn's grandparents wanted to live in the boondocks when his grandfather made his living in town? You did say he was a lawyer, right?"

"One of the best, but he also owned one of the largest cattle ranches around these parts. What's this?"

I glanced over. "*It*, and the one on my side, locks the top of the car in place.… Too bad the place isn't still in operation. I've never seen a real, live, working ranch before."

"Well, you're about to." She pointed to my left.

Our headlights reflected against a white boarded fence. It stretched on for two miles before Quinn signaled and turned. Deciduous trees lined a narrow road, their limbs forming a canopy to a circle drive in front of a well-lit, white, two-story house.

"Is someone here?" I asked Elizabeth after scanning the area for other vehicles.

She shrugged. "Not that I know of. Why?"

I reluctantly reached for the key. "All the lights."

"Just be glad we don't have to stumble around in the dark." She unfolded herself from the car. "Are you coming?"

"I guess," I answered, but she'd already shut her door and was saying something to Quinn, who'd begun to pull our luggage from the bed of his truck.

He handed me my suitcase once I finally joined them. "You girls go ahead and make yourselves at home while I finish unloading all this stuff."

I wanted to ask, what stuff? Or peek over the side of his truck. Instead, I followed Elizabeth up the steps to a roomy wooden porch swathing the width of the house. Rough wooden posts held its roof.

Inside, high-polished hardwood floors reflected the furnishing clear to the kitchen. Plush area rugs snuggled into them, adding warmth. Etched windowpanes gazed down from above the interior doors, making the already oversized doors stand taller, stretching toward the ten-inch crown molding outlining the twelve-foot ceilings. Beyond the swinging butler door, whitewashed kitchen cabinets materialize, right out of the Depression years I'd only seen in *Time* magazine. While to the rear of the house, chocolate-brown leather chairs and matching sofa cozied up before the huge fireplace, lending the family room a manly touch. And the stairs…

I traced the handrail's polished redwood grain. "Not a hint of dust."

"What was that, Mamie?" Elizabeth peered at me from the landing.

Before I could answer, the phone rang, sending her in a flutter. "I'll get it!" She dropped her suitcase and bolted past me. "It's probably Christopher."

I opened my mouth to ask the obvious question, but Quinn elbowed through the front door balancing a box and tripped over a garment bag.

"That's everything." He righted himself and stepped over the blue luggage identical to the one at the top of the stairs.

"Not quite." I stopped shy of the last two steps so we'd be eye level. "Why do I get the impression I've been played?"

"Is something wrong?" His eyes shifted toward Elizabeth slouched in the beige, overstuffed chair with her leg draped over one of its arms.

"Christopher, that's wonderful." She twirled the phone cord around her right index finger, oblivious to the implications of what his calling here meant to me.

"You and Elizabeth planned on me coming here all along, didn't you?"

Quinn flashed a mischievous smile. "We hoped."

"And the bit about you sleeping in the truck, watching out for us? All fabricated to make me feel guilty, right?"

"Not at all." He shifted the box to his other arm. "If you had dug your heels in, then I was prepared to bed down for the night. Or nights. Whatever it took."

I threw my arms out. "This house… It's spotless. No musty smell. Every light in the joint was shining when we drove up. Obviously, Christopher knew to call here. What's the story? Who really lives here? Is this even your grandmother's place?"

Quinn's smile disappeared. "Lacy, the woman who looked after my grandmother while she was alive, still comes once a week. Especially since I'm out here most weekends. I gave her a call earlier today and asked her to make sure everything was ready for guests." He shrugged. "Just in case."

"I'm not angry." How could I be? "I just don't like someone playing games with my emotions."

"And we couldn't stand the thought of you being by yourself with Aaron still out there."

Long before tonight, Quinn and Elizabeth had proven themselves to be the best friends I'd ever known. "Thanks. But you said yourself, he'd probably left town." However, just being back at the cabin had proven to be more than I could've ever imagined.

Quinn furrowed his eyebrows. "I said he *might* have left town."

My heart rate kicked up a notch. "So, what are you trying to say?"

"I got a call from Gary earlier today. Seems Aaron called the hospital during the night, all full of meanness and threats. It shook Tammy up enough to make her confide in the nurse on duty, who called the police. Gary has reason to believe Aaron might still be close by."

I stood there shaking my head, wondering when this nightmare would end. "Did you let Murt and Bud know?"

"Bud and Lily were out feeding the animals, but I told Murt. She said she and Bud won't let anything happen to Lily or Brent and Tammy. I guess the doctor's planning to discharge Brent sometime tomorrow, and they'll all be staying there for now. She also invited the three of us to dinner one day next week. I told her you'd let her know."

I no longer looked at Quinn. I didn't want him to see the fear I knew my eyes reflected. "That's nice."

"There's more, Mamie."

What more could he possibly have to say?

"Your dad's here. In Mountain Home."

A laugh escaped my throat. "*Right*. My dad has no idea where I am. How could he? When I left Mississippi, I had no idea where I was headed or that a place called Mountain Home even existed. And I've made no contact with anyone back there."

"Seems he filed a Missing Person's report with the Clarksdale, Mississippi police department when you never returned home the day of your mother's funeral."

"There's got to be some kind of mistake. My dad doesn't give a hoot about me. He never has. Besides, I left him a note letting him know I wouldn't be back."

"According to your dad—"

"Wait a minute. You talked to him?"

"He stopped by the police station. Gary says he's staying at the Holiday Inn."

The room began to spin. I gripped the handrail and eased myself to the third step. "I don't understand."

"From what I'm told, when you left without saying a word, your father became concerned. At first, he thought you were just distraught about your mother's death. But when you never came home, when he didn't have a clue what had happened, he got worried. He reported you as missing."

This had to be some kind of joke. Aaron's way of trying to find me, maybe, but not… "How do we know it was really my dad?"

"William B. Carlson, five feet ten, black hair, born September 3, 1940. Sound familiar?"

I leaned my head against the railing. "How did he find me?"

"According to Gary, your dad's Missing Person report popped up when they ran a background check on you the morning we filed charges against Aaron."

"I don't understand…why would he run a background check on me? I'm not the guilty party."

"Gary had no way of knowing that without digging deeper. One thing triggered another, I guess. With you not being a minor, there was no reason for the Clarksdale police to contact your dad, so I'm thinking more than likely your father has a crony with the police department, who tipped him off. Whatever the case, your dad's here, and he wants to see you."

I shook my head. "No."

"If he's determined, he won't leave town until he does. It

wouldn't take much to find out where you work, so it might be easier to face him in a neutral place. Of course, I'll be glad to take you and be there if you need me. Just tell me what you want to do.... Mamie?"

Chapter 26

My gut churned over seeing my father again. Even this morning's coffee threatened to revolt.

"Maybe after your mother's death and you leaving, your daddy realized his mistakes and wants nothing more than to apologize," Elizabeth offered last night after I shared why Quinn and I would not be attending the singles group with her and Christopher.

But I had promised to try my best to make it to the worship service. So here I stood, eyeing my two dresses hanging in the empty closet of the bedroom I'd slept in. Neither of them worthy of making a grand first impression.

After wasting as much time dressing as I dared, I headed for the stairs. Halfway down, I spotted Quinn standing next to the couch, dressed in a pair of khakis and a casual blue-on-blue striped shirt with a button-down collar. Perhaps the members at Mountain Home's First Baptist were much less formal than I'd suspected, or maybe he was simply dressing down for my benefit. After all, he'd seen enough of my wardrobe to know either my lack of taste in clothes or my pocketbook hindered me when it came to the latest styles.

"It makes a great sliding board."

"Excuse me."

"The rails. I used to slide down them every chance I got."

Instantly, in my mind's eye, I pictured Quinn, Lily's age, flying backward down the sturdy mahogany banister. "Only when your grandmother wasn't looking, I bet."

"Actually, she didn't mind. Said it made one less thing for her to dust. However, the day she caught me using one of the sofa cushions as a sled and the stairs as a snow-covered mountain," he chuckled, "well, let's just say she wasn't amused."

I settled in one of the nearby chairs. "What happened?"

"It was everything a rambunctious kid could hope for: fast, scary, and unpredictable. With every step, I bounced higher and held on tighter. Expecting to stop once I reached the bottom, you can imagine my surprise when I kept going. Clean across the living room floor and into Nana's whatnot table."

"Yikes."

"Yep. There I was sprawled out with glass all around me and Nana standing over me, madder than I'd ever seen her. Once she realized I wasn't hurt, she jerked me up and threatened to dust the seat of my britches with the flyswatter, if she ever caught me pulling such an 'idiotic stunt' again. Of course, I knew I was in no real danger of corporal punishment, but it didn't come as any surprise when she sentenced me to pulling weeds in her flower garden for the rest of the afternoon."

"So did you...? Ever bobsled down the stairs again?"

Quinn chose a chair next to mine. "Not a chance. I never could stand disappointing Nana. She was the best... sweet, could throw a baseball, taught me how to fish and swim—"

"And cook," I interrupted.

"That, too." He smiled and picked at the crease in his pants.

"You miss her...your nana."

With a deep breath, Quinn looked around. "This house. The memories. If I listen real hard, I can still hear her laughter. She was *always* laughing." His eyes crinkled as if seeing her once again. "Yeah, I miss her."

"What was your grandfather like?"

"Pop?" His smile widened. "He was a big guy with a big heart, who could hold his own in any courtroom. If you didn't know him, you might be intimidated by his baritone and gruffness. But he was gentle. He loved his family and absolutely adored Nana. They had a wonderful marriage…. Fifty-two years, and he still lit up whenever she walked in the room. The two of them held hands like a couple of teenagers while watching TV or sitting in the porch swing. Nana used to say every woman should know the kind of love and respect Pop showed her. They had a marriage most people only dreamed of. The kind too few are willing to hold out for… Or work on."

My curiosity stirred. "You make marriage sound like a chore."

"I think it can be, if you don't choose the right person. Especially if both husband and wife fail to put God first. That's why you pray long before you ever meet Miss Right…or in your case, Mr. Right. Pop often said marriage was something you had to work at constantly if you wanted it to last. Each person has to decide what they want to bring to the marriage and place it in a joint wagon, so to speak. Be willing to pull while the other one pushed, so no one is carrying the full load. To know there might be times when one of you had to get in and rest: Like when one is sick. There might even be times when both had to get in and rest, 'so be willing to throw some stuff out of your wagon, son,' he used to tell me."

I couldn't help but wonder if Quinn's grandfather had known Memaw, or if all old people talked in riddles when it came to marriage? I shook my head, trying to dislodge thoughts of happily ever after. Believing in fairy tales could only bring heartache.

"Are y'all ready?" Miss Style, herself, sashayed down the stairs. A bright orange skirt flared from her hips and hit mid-calf. A cream-colored, silk blouse sported the Dynasty fad—shoulder pads. Elizabeth paused at the bottom stair, eyeing us reclining in the living room. Her tapping foot sent the orange skirt bouncing. "I promised to meet Christopher in front of the church no later than a quarter till eleven."

Here I sat, less than ten minutes after dropping Elizabeth off, stirring a cup of coffee I knew I wouldn't drink, waiting for Daddy to answer my question, "Why are you here?"

He glanced at his watch, over my right shoulder, over his—everywhere but at me—while fumbling for his cigarettes. "You left so suddenly, Mamie. What was I to think?"

"I'm sure you saw the note I wrapped around the bottle of booze under your truck seat. Now whether you were in the state of mind to read it or not—"

"Don't be disrespectful." He snapped. "Nobody likes a smart-aleck kid."

Business was picking up inside the Holiday Inn restaurant, enough to keep Daddy's brute strength at bay. Plus, Quinn sat two tables over. "You never have cared about me—or Mama, as far as I could tell—so forgive me for being a little cynical about your sudden fatherly interest."

"Look, I didn't come here to fight with you. I just wanted to make sure you were all right and," he opened the folder setting on the table, "to let you know I'm selling the home place."

"Wow." I jolted slightly. "Kinda sudden, isn't it?"

"You're grown now. I don't figure you'll ever be moving back in. Your mother's gone. There're too many memories in that old house. Most of them bad." He pushed the legal-looking paper my direction and set a black pen on top of it. "So why not?" He pointed his stubby finger at the line above my typed name.

Silverware clattered against the floor nearby. A waitress rushed over to pick it up and was saying something to Quinn. Ignoring her, he locked eyes with me and gave his head a subtle shake.

"What happens if I don't sign?"

"Makes no difference to me." Daddy leaned back and took a drag from his cigarette. "The place is mine to do with as I choose. I paid for it. We both know your mother never worked a day in her life."

"She washed and ironed your clothes, cooked your meals, and raised me. You don't call that work?"

"What's the big deal? Women I know do all *that* and hold down a good-paying job."

Part of me wanted to throw my now-lukewarm coffee in his face. Instead, I pushed my chair back and gathered my purse.

He grabbed my wrist. "Where do you think you're going?"

Before I had a chance to answer, Quinn towered over Daddy with his hand on Dad's shoulder. "You might want to let go of her."

"Look, friend, this has nothing to do with you."

Free from Dad's grip, I pulled on Quinn's arm. "Let's go."

"Oh, I get it." Daddy roared with laughter. "You two know one another. Makes me wonder just how well you know my daughter, boy."

Quinn placed his hand on the small of my back and steered me away from the table.

"Don't let her get her claws in you, boy," Dad shouted for all to hear. "You'll never be the same."

Before I could stop Quinn, he whirled around and got in Dad's face. "The only reason you're still sitting in that chair, old man, is because my mother taught me to always be kind to my elders. But my grandmother taught me to not *ever* allow *anyone* to mistreat a lady. So if I were you, I'd keep my mouth shut and go back where you came from."

Dad smiled and held his hands up, palms out. "Okay, okay, but not until she signs some papers. I don't want her coming back on me in the future trying to stake a claim on anything I've got."

"Mamie's not going to sign anything without having her lawyer take a look at it first." Quinn pulled out one of his cards and slapped it in front of Dad, then picked up the file and placed it under his arm. "I'm sure he'll be in touch."

Chapter 27

I balled my hands into fists, angry at myself for letting my father get to me. "He's never going to leave town until he gets what he came for."

Quinn placed his key in the ignition but didn't turn it. Instead, he opened the file laying between us. "Well, let's just see exactly what he's after."

He studied the papers briefly before asking, "Do you know if your mother had a will?"

"She never said one way or the other, but I'd have to say no. Why?"

"Then your father may have been telling the truth. These papers have been drawn up to protect his interest."

"In what?"

"Money, the house… Anything the courts might ascertain could be rightly yours since your mother did not have a will. *If* you wanted to challenge him."

"Why would I want to do that when all I ever wanted was to be free of him?"

Quinn's right eyebrow rose. "What would your mother want?"

"For me to be happy."

"What about any memorabilia? Family heirlooms? He could sell everything, and you'd get nothing. Are you sure you want to walk away empty-handed?"

With more sarcasm than humor, I laughed. "What family heirlooms? Our house is nothing grand. Most of the furniture has seen better days. Mom never owned expensive jewelry. I've already taken the things I wanted." Just this morning I'd opened the Ziploc bag holding two of her handkerchiefs, touched the fabric that had touched her, and inhaled the smell uniquely hers—Pond's cream and violets. "The rest I gave to a friend of hers, to keep Dad from throwing them out with the trash. The main thing Mom gave me, I have tucked away in my heart for all the years to come… Memories of a mother's love." I snatched a renegade tear from my cheek. "That's worth much more than a house or a bank account."

Quinn handed me his handkerchief. "And you didn't have that with your dad?"

"Never."

"His loss." He reached for my hand. "Tell me what you want to do."

"I'll sign the paper."

"You want to wait and think on it a few days?"

"No." I shook my head. "He can have it all. I don't care. He just needs to leave me alone."

"Okay." Leaning past me, he opened the glove box and retrieved a pen. "I'll make sure he gets the message."

"Thanks, but I imagine you've seen enough of William Bernard Carlson for one day. I'll go."

"We'll both go," he insisted.

What was it about this guy? "I bet you've asked yourself a million times—as big as Norfork Lake is, why that spot and that moment?"

His dimple flashed my way. "What are you talking about?"

"The day we first met. I mean, if you hadn't decided to go diving that day or surface when you did, we never would've met, and you wouldn't be tangled up in all this mess of me, my dad, or Aaron Holbrook."

That now-familiar hint of mischief sparkled in his eyes. "One of these days, I'll tell you about a guy who noticed a good-looking redhead sitting on a dock and how he managed to get her attention. But first, we've got a document to deliver."

Even though Quinn and I didn't expect to find Daddy still in the dining area, we decided to look there before asking the desk clerk for his room number. Quinn knew the guy on duty, of course, which made things less complicated. By the time we stood outside Dad's room, if not for Quinn by my side, I would've slipped the folder under the door and walked away. Instead, I held my chin up, my shoulders back, and knocked.

"Coming."

My heart slammed against my lungs at the sound of a woman's voice. "I can't do this." I turned to leave, but not before Gloria Talbert stood only inches away.

"Mamie!" Gloria stepped toward me with her arms out. "It's so good to see you."

I backed away. "Please don't do that."

Her arms fell to her side. She eyed Quinn. "Y'all want to come in? Your father's in the bathroom."

It took everything in me to remain calm. "Make sure you give this to Dad." I handed her the folder.

"Mamie, I hope you know, I'd never try to take your mother's place."

The desire to pull Gloria's bleach-blonde hair out by the roots or to walk away battled within as if two dogs were fighting for first place.

The Glorias in mine and Mama's life had been many, but the one standing in front of me would be my last.

"You could never take my mom's place. She was kind, good, and decent. A lady who, for whatever reason, stayed with her husband and never went after someone else's. She loved God, me, and—I suppose at one point, if not always—my father." I swallowed hard. "She's gone now, so I guess he's all yours."

I spun on my heels and headed for the exit sign at the end of the hallway. Not until I reached the truck did I emit a relieved sigh.

Moments later, we pulled out of the Holiday Inn parking lot. "Are you okay?" Quinn asked.

"Not completely…but I will be." I rolled down my window and turned my face into the wind.

"You want to get something to drink?"

I slid my gaze in his direction. "Elizabeth's expecting us at church, remember?" Besides, I needed something…anything…to take my mind off what just happened.

"She's probably already figured we aren't going to make it, but if that's what you want to do… We'll be a little late."

"Good, with any luck, we'll forgo meet-and-greet, if your church is in to that."

"They are." He chuckled.

The chorus of "How Great Thou Art" greeted us as Quinn and I entered the church auditorium. To my disappointment, all the back pews were full. Several pairs of eyes inspected us as he ushered me down the aisle, his hand warming the small of my back. Thankfully, a man and the woman standing next to him made room for us midway. When she handed me her opened songbook, I smiled and thanked her. When she stretched past me for Quinn's extended hand,

I gave the middle-aged couple a second look and almost slid under the pew. The woman's dark-chocolate eyes with specks of gold, the man's square jaw, six-foot frame, wide shoulders, and peppered *black* hair…

With shaky hands, I shoved the book toward Quinn and closed my eyes, trying to imagine what I'd say to his parents once the service ended. What would they say when they found out I'd moved into Nana's?

"You may be seated," a man in front announced.

How about "you're dismissed"? I mentally screamed.

Quinn leaned over and whispered, "You're in for a treat."

No sooner had he spoken than Susie slipped out of the choir loft and crossed over to the podium. Too self-absorbed in my own woes, I'd failed to notice her earlier. The congregation hushed as she held the microphone and nodded. At once, the rich sound of an orchestra flowed from the speakers, followed by an amazingly powerful voice that didn't match the petite, five-foot-two, blonde beauty. With compassion, Susie sang of God's unfailing love and forgiveness. With control, her soprano voice reminded me of a clear stream skipping over rocks, then gliding into nearby pools as she gave thanks for all the trials God had brought her through, even when she'd turned her back on Him.

The thought of Susie deliberately doing anything to hurt anyone, much less God, was hard for me to imagine. But I couldn't help but wonder if she saw her diabetes as one of the trials she sang of and— if it was true—how she could give thanks for a disease that could send her into a crippling stupor without warning. At least, that's what happened on the way to Memaw's.

Then I remembered Mom's words the day I expressed anger at God for not healing her body of cancer. "God allows us to go through things in our life," she said, "but He never allows us to go through them without being there to hold us up. Don't be angry at God," she added. "Grow in whatever hardships come your way, my sweet girl."

I squeezed my eyes shut, trying to hold back a barrage of tears. *I'm tired of hurting and being hurt, Lord, and I'm tired of being angry. Help me. Forgive me.*

Quinn had hardly introduced me to his parents when others began to come by, introducing themselves and bombarding me with questions.

"You're not from around here, are you?"

"What brought you to Mountain Home?"

"Where are you from?"

"Aren't you the girl who works at M&H?"

But when Jeremy, a sandy-haired tyke squirming in his mother's arms, pointed at me and asked Quinn, "Is she your girlfriend", a muscle in my cheek twitched as I smiled, trying to camouflage uneasiness.

"Jeremy!" the youngster's mother scolded.

"If I were you, I'd answer the question before some ridiculous rumor starts flying around about you two."

I turned toward the voice behind me. Janie, with her arms crossed and grinning like a Cheshire cat, eyed Quinn. Thankfully, a friendly face stood next to her.

"It's been my experience that anyone who's prone to spread a little homegrown gossip never lets a simple thing like truth stand in the way." Doris nudged her way around Janie and threw her arms around me. "How you doing, sugar?"

My lips quivered. I didn't dare speak as I clung to Doris, the first caring person I ran into after Mama's death. The person, who flipped a coin and talked of paradise, who intrigued me to investigate and invest myself in Mountain Home. The woman whose husband taught me all I needed to know to land a job at M&H. The very person I'd been thinking of all week and desperately needed right now.

Chapter 28

Quinn and Elizabeth insisted Doris and I spend the afternoon without them. "Just be careful," Quinn stated. "Don't go to the cabin. Be aware of your surroundings." He slipped one of his business cards in my hand. "The address and phone number for my apartment are on the back. Call me if you need *anything*."

"What was that all about?" Doris asked as we wove around parked cars, looking for her white Pinto. "Is he afraid the brunette—who obviously can't stand you, but adores your Mr. Wonderful—might track you down and do a number on you?"

"First of all, Quinn and I are nothing more than friends. And, yes, he's worried, but not about Janie. The brunette." I eyed her across the roof of her car. "How did you find me, anyway? I've never mentioned First Baptist in any of my letters." Why would I? I'd never been here, or to any of the other churches in town, before today.

"A God thing, I guess. After I went by your address and couldn't find you, I came here. The church I always attend when I'm in town." She speared me with a look of concern. "But don't try to change the subject."

After I slid into the passenger's seat, Brent's injuries, Lily, Aaron breaking into the cabin and snatching me out the bathroom window, the police, my dad, Gloria, Quinn and Elizabeth and me staying at his nana's—the whole kit and caboodle spewed out like an overfilled pressure cooker. Until, exhausted, I grabbed my purse and followed her into the diner.

"Thank God for Quinn and Elizabeth! I don't know how you've held up through all this and managed to hold down a job." After ordering, Doris leaned across the table at Gina's Diner and whispered, "Sugar, you need a gun."

I shook my head, even though I'd thought about it more than once since the break in. "I don't know anything about guns. Besides, Quinn says it's a matter of time before the police catch Aaron." He also expressed early on his doubts of Aaron still being around. "Who knows?" I attempted to wash down my doubt of this nightmare ever ending, with a long drink of iced tea.

"Tell you what…" She smiled and waited until the waitress finished refilling our glasses. "Why don't you come work for me at the diner? Move in with me and Barry until you find a place of your own."

"Thanks." The offer was tempting. "I really mean it."

"Good." She turned her attention back to her food.

"But I can't."

Her fork clanked against her plate. "Why not?"

"It's hard to explain." I shrugged. "I just can't."

"Are you worried Aaron might follow you?"

"Not really."

"If it's work, your boss will understand. If not, then too bad."

The thought of giving up my job made me ill. "It's not that."

"Aw…" Doris bit her lip. "The love for one man outweighs the fear of another. No wonder the brunette worked herself in a snit. She doesn't stand a dog's chance with you around."

Quinn had proven himself to be kind, giving, protective, an all-around good guy. I only hoped one day he and I could be as close friends as he and Elizabeth. "Janie has nothing to worry about. He and I are just friends."

"Then why? If you're not crazy in love, what's holding you here?"

"If anyone had asked that question days ago, hours ago, even, my answer would've been based on stubborn determination and bitterness."

"And now?"

"It's strange. I left Mississippi and all the hurtful memories. So I thought. Most of them followed me here. Some literally. There're reasons to leave here, yet something tells me this is where I'm meant to be. Good or bad."

"Are you saying you've found home?"

"I'm saying I've got to see where this life takes me."

Four days later, I stood outside the paint-worn farmhouse with Quinn and Elizabeth, eager to see the two young towheads who'd forever hold a special place in my heart.

"Mamie's here!"

Lily grabbed my hand and pulled me forward. It was the first time I'd seen her smile, her hair clean and combed, and her wearing something other than rags. "Look, Brent, it's Mamie."

For a brief moment, I blinked away disbelief. Rather than a lifeless, pale child, a grinning Brent, his rosy cheeks bunched upward, pulled his arms from under the patchwork quilt. I knelt beside the sofa and placed my face next to his—just to make sure his healthy-looking skin color wasn't due to fever—and absorbed his affections.

"Don't squeeze her too hard, Champ." Bud teased before encouraging Elizabeth and Quinn to have a seat. "Grandmaw Murt and Tammy are stirring in the kitchen. They'll be out in a minute."

"I'll see if they can use some help, but first," Elizabeth knelt beside me, "someone needs to introduce me to this good-looking young man."

Brent giggled, holding his hand over his stomach.

Lily tapped me on my shoulder. "Who are those for?"

I followed the direction of her slender finger. I'd forgotten about the gifts Quinn had retrieved from the truck bed…the ones we'd purchased earlier at one of the local hardware stores. "They're presents for you and Brent."

"Whose is whose?" Quinn teased, searching the wrapped packages. "I don't see a name anywhere."

Lily scrambled to her feet. "If we don't find a name, I bet the pink one's mine and the blue one's Brent's."

"Only one way to do this." Quinn held the two gifts out. "You pick."

She took them both. "I better give Brent his, since Mama don't want him running around."

No longer interested in playing bashful, Brent tore at the blue spaceman print.

"What'd you get?" Lily squealed, equally excited as her brother.

"Cars. Bunches and bunches of 'em."

Hopefully, the gift Elizabeth and I had picked for Lily rated as high as Quinn's choice for Brent. We didn't have to wait long.

"A Barbie doll! Mama, look." Lily sprinted toward Murt and the dishwater blonde as the two walked into the room.

Tall, and much too thin, Lily's mother brushed her daughter's hair back. "That's real nice, honey."

"Look at mine, Mama." Brent waved several cars in his small fists.

His mother nodded and offered her son a faint smile. "I see them."

"Tammy," Murt wrapped an arm around her granddaughter's

waist and nudged her forward, "I want you to meet these good people."

I stood and reached for Tammy's hand. The roughness of her palms took me by surprise. No doubt they matched her harsh life with Aaron Holbrook.

"Thank you…For taking up with my children." Tammy kept her head bowed, only occasionally giving me a peek into her lifeless blue eyes.

According to Bud, Tammy had had a wonderful life with her husband, the father of Lily and Brent. How long had it taken Aaron to break her? To instill a fear most people had never experienced, much less understood. But I did, and after one scary encounter and a threat, "I'm not done with you," I did even more.

My hope was that someday Tammy and I could share something much greater…friendship.

Weeks later, I brushed off the bottom step and sat with my back against the cool concrete of the next one up, enjoying the bitter flavor of my first cup of coffee of the day. The sun had begun its morning climb, casting gold across the sky's massive expanse. Hardly the picture of promised rain. Shoots of grass waved from the warm breeze more like early summer than spring.

"Good morning." Quinn stood in the doorway in his sock feet, Levi's, and white T-shirt. "Mind if I join you?"

Why would anyone so stinking good looking not have a dozen girls chasing after him? "Sure." I scooted over to make room.

He took a swig of his coffee before settling next to me. "What's got you up so early?"

"Um." I shrugged, inhaling the fresh menthol, woody scent I'd recently discovered came from a bottle. Aqua Velva aftershave. "Thinking, mostly."

"Having second thoughts about signing your dad's papers?"

I gripped my mug tighter. "Not at all."

Quinn's right eyebrow shot up. "You sure?"

"Look." I tossed the remainder of my coffee on a nearby bush. "Not that I could ever forget, but it's kinda hard to be reminded of your dad's selfishness and infidelity. Especially when she's standing right in front of you. So am I angry about that…? Yes. About relinquishing something I never owned…?" I snorted. "Not hardly."

"Mamie, you've been through a lot. The death of your mother. A major move. New job. New friends. Then this mess with Aaron…" He stretched his legs out in front him. "I've always had my family's love and support, so it's hard for me to imagine what it would be like not to have them in my life. Unlike your situation, my dad and I are extremely close…as are Mom and I. It would be so easy to become hardened. Even cynical." He snaked his hand over and locked his little finger around mine. "You're afraid. I get that. You've been hurt. I get that, too, and I don't ever want to see you hurt again. But don't allow pain and distrust to steal your joy and rob you of the life God wants you to have. Don't let people like your dad and Aaron dictate your future and pull you down."

In times past, I would've argued. After all, Quinn admitted it. He didn't know what it was like to have a father like mine. It wasn't his mother who died. Instead, I reflected on his words. Far too long I'd been tainted by my daddy's cruelty and lack of respect toward Mom, me, and women in general. Men like Aaron were Satan's tools, used to reinforce the attitude I'd developed early in life. "You're right. I'm just not sure how to erase the pain and stop the anger overnight."

"With God's help, you take it one day at a time. Some days moment by moment until the day you wake up and realize you're free. Self-destructive people from your past no longer have a hold on you, and forgiveness replaces anger. Even wonderful memories of your mother will outweigh the unbearable sadness of her death." He brushed an escaped tear from my cheek with his thumb. "Meanwhile, I think an afternoon on the lake fishing might be just what the two of us need."

Trying my hand at fishing had been something I'd looked forward to since Doris mentioned it the first day we met. "Today?"

"Why not?"

Had he forgotten what day it was? "It's Sunday."

"I don't think God'll mind. We'll hook up the boat, pack a lunch, and take off right after second service."

"Don't you think we should check with Elizabeth first?"

"Check with me about what?" Yawning and disheveled, Elizabeth nudged the back door open with her hip while blowing steam from the oversized mug cupped between her hands.

"Taking the boat out this afternoon and doing some fishing."

"Oh no." She waved. "Christopher would love it, but I don't intend to spend the first Sunday after a long tax season threading worms on a hook. Count us out."

The thought of Elizabeth not going unnerved me. I'd never been on a date-type outing—alone with a guy. Not that this would be a date. I hopped to my feet. "I don't have a license."

"Not a problem. Any of the bait shops sell them." Quinn tilted his head, waiting, and I was out of excuses.

In spite of the familiar voice in my head that screamed "run" anytime a guy attempted to get too close, the desire to do something more than work, eat, sleep, and look over my shoulder overruled. "Okay. You're on."

Chapter 29

Instead of the pontoon, Quinn decided to take his grandfather's jon boat. A good thing, since he gave me the choice of backing his truck halfway into the water or driving the aluminum three seater off the trailer.

Three men on the nearby dock watched in amusement as Quinn reviewed the instructions while unhooking the last security strap. "Remember, twist the handle to the left to go faster, to the right slows it down. Unlike steering a car, if you want to go right, push the handle left, and vice versa." Then he hopped back in his truck and began the descent down the long concrete ramp.

When the exhaust from truck's tailpipe began sputtering water, I yelled and grabbed both sides of the boat, sure in a matter of inches the whole truck would slip into the lake. Right before I could go into a full-blown state of panic, the truck stopped, and the boat began to float. Taking one of the paddles, I pushed against the trailer's frame until the *Mad Mama*—the christened name by the owner before Pop, according to Quinn—cleared.

"I'll meet you at the dock," Quinn yelled and waved before leaving me to navigate out of the way of the next group waiting to launch.

"You want me to tie you up, little lady?"

The words *honey, baby, darling, sweetheart,* or *angel* from the lips of any man left a sour taste in my mouth, but these words, along with the sinister smile on this buffoon's face infuriated me.

Remembering the Scripture the pastor read just minutes ago, "*Let no unwholesome word proceed from your mouth*", and something about giving words for edification, had me clamping down on the rebuke burning the tip of my tongue. Instead, I smiled and said, "I'm not sure if I'll be staying." One more smart-aleck remark from him, and I wouldn't. "But thank you."

More than ready to relinquish my position as captain of the ship, I exhaled my relief when Quinn arrived. Only one problem. With a cooler, life jackets, a minnow bucket, tackle box, our rods, and other paraphernalia blocking me from the seat on the other end, I had to crawl out and then back into the wobbly boat. Without Quinn's assurance and strong grip, I'm not so sure I wouldn't have gone for an unwanted dip.

"We're off," he announced once we got settled. He pushed away from the dock and headed out to the open lake with more speed than I thought the old *Mad Mama* had in her.

The wind from the speed threatened to snatch Nana's borrowed straw hat from my head, even with my hand firmly holding it in place.

"You want me to slow down?"

"No." I giggled with a sense of adventure. If anything, I wanted him to go faster.

As if he read my mind, he bumped it up a notch, leaving a V-shaped wake of white foam boiling behind us. I dipped the tips of my fingers into the water, causing droplets of coolness to splatter against my arms, legs, and face.

"We're almost there," Quinn hollered over the motor's roar and nodded toward an outcrop of rocks along the right shoreline.

Minutes later, he brought the boat to a crawl. "Are you hungry?"

He had insisted on taking care of everything himself, including packing our lunch while I scrambled to dress for church and pick out clothes for our outing. We'd stopped by the cabin to retrieve my ratty Keds. "Whenever you are."

Just shy of his claimed favorite spot to fish, Quinn tied the boat's rope to a tree limb. I hadn't realized how thirsty I'd become until he pulled two bottled Cokes dripping with water and chips of ice from the cooler and handed me one. The sweet drink fizzed and burned as I took several large, satisfying gulps.

"I thought you might need to eat before getting your hands all grungy with worm guts and slimy fish scales. I, on the other hand," he passed me a partial roll of paper towel, "find that a little lake water, a halfway-clean spot on my jeans, and I'm good to go."

"Yuck. I think I just lost my appetite."

"Aaaah." He held up his right index finger. "I have just the cure. Chocolate, marshmallow, and graham crackers."

"S'mores?" Either this man loved chocolate as much as I did, or he'd certainly zeroed in on my number-one weakness. However, with all the underbrush and rocks, I didn't see the ideal spot to build a fire.

"The next best thing." He flipped the cooler lid back again and presented a couple of double-decker Moon Pies. "I figure while we're eating the main course, we can lay these babies out and let the sun act as our campfire."

I was for skipping the meal and going straight for the dessert, but for curiosity's sake, I pointed at the red ice chest. "What else you got in there?"

"In sticking with the flavors no child ever outgrows, we have chips and your choice of either peanut butter and grape jelly or grape jelly and peanut butter sandwiches."

Only when I noticed Quinn's smile flat-line, did I realize my recently acquired dislike of peanut butter must be flashing across my face like today's headline in the *Baxter Bulletin*.

"Is it the grape jelly? We can probably scrape most of it off."

"No. In fact, grape's one of my favorites. It's just… How would you feel if, in keeping with your theme, I had my dessert first?"

His smile quickly returned. "Whatever makes you happy, Miss Eisenhower. I just want you to have a great day."

"You're a pro." Quinn strung my tenth catch of the day onto the blue nylon stringer tied to the boat. "Are you sure you've never done this before?"

He was teasing, and we both knew it. He'd spent so much time untangling my line from tree limbs and brush tops that he'd hardly fished himself. To make matters worse, I didn't have it in me to stab a poor minnow through its tail. And the worms! Night crawlers, Quinn called them, looked more like snakes. I couldn't even make myself take my fish off. The first one had teeth like a piranha. Not that I'd ever seen one. Quinn called it a walleye and bragged about their taste. I'd have to take his word for it.

"Why don't we reel in and mosey around the next bend? I've got one more spot I want to show you before we head back."

We didn't have to go far. The small sandless beach with one protruding boulder off to the side begged to be explored. Quinn ran the nose of the boat close to the shore, then jumped out and offered me his hand. "Out of all the places, this one's probably my favorite," he said, making sure I had my footing before he let go. "Pop and I used to come here to fish, swim, cook hot dogs."

"And climb rocks?" I interrupted.

"As well as throw them." He finished securing the boat, and then searched the ground. "They have to be flat. The flatter the better." He picked up one and rubbed his thumb over it before effortlessly sending the rock skipping across the glassy water.

I'd heard it could be done, but I had never witnessed the feat firsthand. "Do it again."

"It's all in the wrist. Here." He selected another rock for himself and one for me, allowing me to examine their smooth surfaces. Next, he showed me how to circle my index finger around the outer edges while gripping the stone in place with my thumb. "Bend your knees, so when you throw, the rock will be parallel to the water. Flex your wrist all the way back, then snap it forward, and release like so." Again, his stone skipped multiple times across the open water, while mine broke the surface with a plunk and sank.

Quinn kept feeding me small ones, larger ones, giving me pointers, praising my form. My wrist ached.

"You can do this," he encouraged.

I put all my weight on my right foot and leaned to the right, my shoulders almost parallel to the ground, and snapped the rock toward the water.

"I did it." I whirled around, hoping Quinn hadn't missed my small accomplishment. "It only bounced once, but I did it."

"You sure did." Quinn beamed, his eyes fixed on mine causing my pulse to bolt, taking my breath with it.

He stepped closer. "Do you have any idea how much I enjoy being with you? Watching you smile. Listening to you laugh."

I tried to gather my thoughts. Wondered what to say.

"A timid, beautiful redhead intrigued me that first day I saw you at the docks. A fiery dame who threatened to knock my head off a few days later sent me into a state of confusion. But the night we ate under the stars in front of the cabin, you stole my heart, Miss Eisenhower."

Wanting desperately to deny my own feelings, I looked away, but Quinn placed his finger under my chin and gently guided my face back to his. "I know you trust me, or you never would've come out here with me today…"

Right now, it was me I didn't trust. I'd never planned on letting my guard down with any guy. How did this happen?

"…and I know you care for me. All I ask is that you give *us* a chance."

Panic twisted my insides. Fear threatened to smother me. But my heart begged to be released from the hard shell of protection I'd spent years building.

"Please." His eyes probed mine and waited for an answer.

Chapter 30

With his thumb, Quinn traced the edges of my lower lip, waiting for my answer.

A storm of emotions raged, pitting my heart against my mind. For a moment, I almost knocked his hand away.

"I do love you," he whispered.

Never had I imagined hearing those words from any man. A lightning bolt of fear sliced through me, rendering me speechless.

"Trust your heart, Mamie."

I wanted to, but—

"Trust me," he pleaded.

Stubbornness thundered one more shot, reminding me of my parents' failures, but my feelings for Quinn would no longer stay safely tucked away in some quiet dark corner. Unable to speak, I nodded. So slightly, I couldn't be sure he'd notice. My face flamed as he leaned closer. His lips brushed mine, sending ripples of chills throughout my body. I drank in the warmth of his touch and struggled with the unexplainable desire to scream and laugh.

My lips tingled, wanting more.

Jim waved his hand in front of my face. "Did you get hit on the head again, Mamie?"

Yesterday's events vanished. "What?"

"You're moving slower than a ninety-year-old woman with a broken arm. Are you sick?"

"Noooo," I answered, frustrated with myself, embarrassed I'd been caught reliving the private moment between me and Quinn.

"Then you better get a move on before Dave gets his hackles up." Jim motioned toward two tubs of ground chuck that weren't at my station earlier. "The only reason he hasn't already had a fit is because you came in early."

Thirty minutes early to be exact. I'd spent half the night thinking about Quinn…us. Giddy one minute. Worried about getting hurt the next. This morning I tried to act normal, as if nothing had happened, but it had. We needed to talk, but all I could do was babble like an idiot. Elizabeth sitting between us at the breakfast table didn't help, and neither did him winking at me whenever she wasn't paying attention.

Jim looked at me through squinted eyes. "Are you sure you're okay?"

I faked a smile. "Positive. So maybe you should get back to work before we both get in trouble."

"Yes, ma'am." He saluted and sauntered toward his workstation.

"Jim?" I snagged his sleeve.

"Yes."

"Thanks."

That afternoon, Jim opened the rear door—ready to walk me to my car—and the two of us stopped in our tracks. Quinn stood at the end of the loading dock with one leg propped on the bottom step.

"You need something, fellow?"

My heart swelled with pride over Jim's protectiveness and, at the same time, skipped a beat at the sight of Quinn. "It's okay. He's a friend."

"Yeah?" Jim's cocky tone, along with his smirk, likely meant I'd have to tolerate unbearable ribbing in the days ahead or, at least, a barrage of questions. "How in the world did you get tangled up with some scrub horse like Quinn Randall?"

Quinn strolled across the dock, laughing, his hand extended. "Man, don't go putting me down in front of Mamie. She might think you're serious."

The two exchanged greetings, asked about each other's family.

Seemed, years back, Jim had dated Quinn's older sister, the blonde beauty.

After a bit, Jim slapped Quinn on the shoulder. "I could stand out here and talk all day, but if I don't get back inside, Dave's going to think something happened to us. We don't want that, do we, Mamie?"

I shook my head. "It wouldn't be in our best interest."

"Mamie told me about you and Dave keeping an eye out for her. I appreciate it."

"No problem."

After saying our goodbyes, Quinn placed his hand to the small of my back and led me to the driver's side of his truck. "I thought we'd grab a couple of hamburgers and drinks if that's okay with you?"

"What about Elizabeth?"

"She won't be home until later tonight. I guess she and Christopher had something planned."

They'd been out every night since tax season ended. Still, I couldn't help but notice the deep lines etched between Quinn's eyes. "Is something wrong? Is everything okay with Elizabeth?"

"Don't worry. She's fine."

My insides began to shake as if they'd turned into Jell-O. "Your words tell me one thing: your face tells me something else. What's going on?"

Quinn held the truck door open. "How about we go get those hamburgers?"

My feet rooted to the ground. "I'm not hungry. And I'm not budging until you tell me what's wrong."

"Let's get in, and I'll tell you everything."

The repulsive face of the man who tormented me in my dreams, almost nightly, flashed across my mind. A wave of nausea followed. "He's here, isn't he?" I asked, sliding across the bench seat. "He got to Brent and Lily."

"They're safe."

"And Tammy?"

"From what I understand," Quinn's voice remained calm, "she's going to be okay."

My fingernails dug into my palms as I fisted my hands. "The monster got to her, didn't he? Why can't the police do something? How long will he get away with hurting people? It has got to—" I bit down on my lip, unable to say another word and keep the tears at bay.

"Come here." Quinn reached over, wrapped his arms around me, and pulled me closer. "He won't hurt anyone ever again. It's over, Mamie."

I looked up. Surely, I'd misunderstood.

"Aaron's dead," he added.

My mind couldn't comprehend Quinn's words. I glanced at my watch, the back door to M&H, my car, trying to get my bearings. Waiting to wake in another panicked stupor.

"Did you hear what I said, Mamie? Do you understand what I'm trying to tell you?"

"How? How did he die?"

"It was an accident."

Bud's words, "sometimes I think about it…killing him," invaded my thoughts.

Almost too afraid to hear the answer, I scooted to face Quinn, wet my lips, then cleared my throat, and somehow managed to speak. "What kind of accident?"

He sandwiched my hands with his. "Apparently, Bud and Lily had already left for school when Tammy went out to hang clothes on the line. She didn't see or hear anything unusual, but then the dog— remember the big black one that took a liking to Lily?—started growling. Tammy got nervous, ran back in the house, and told Murt, who called 911. Before anyone had a chance to get there, Aaron found a way into the basement and made it upstairs unnoticed. They don't know how long he'd been in the house, but when Murt went to check on Brent, Aaron was standing beside his bed."

"You said Brent was okay."

"I said he and Lily were safe…and they are. Brent was a little shook up, but he's all right."

"What about Murt?"

"She took a nasty blow to the head and a fall. From what I understand, the EMTs checked her out and didn't find anything broken. I guess they wanted to take her to the hospital for X-rays, but she refused to leave Brent. Tammy, on the other hand, has a broken jaw and three cracked ribs. She told the police she thought he was going to kill her."

"Why didn't he?"

"The sirens. She said when he heard the sirens he panicked, asked about the keys to the old one-ton farm truck, yanked her to her feet, and drug her outside. She slowed him down, so he left her. By the time he got the truck cranked and pulled out, Gary and his deputies were on his tail. Aaron made the mistake of taking the road we walked in on the night with Lily."

"The ditch?"

"Right. Only I guess he didn't see it until it was too late. The old truck didn't have seatbelts, so with a nosedive into the bank of rock and mud, Aaron went through the windshield."

"You think he might've crashed the truck deliberately?"

"We'll never know. But if so, I don't think he meant for it to end the way it did. I'll spare you the gory details and just tell you he didn't die right away. Nor lose consciousness. Gary, the policeman who took your statement, said he tried to talk to Aaron about his relationship with the Lord, but Aaron wouldn't have any part of it. Cussed his father, God, everyone…including the EMTs when they tried to help. The doctors did what they could. He died at the hospital about an hour ago."

Ashamed for feeling a sense of relief and overwhelmed by Aaron's disregard for life, including his own, I asked, "You wonder what happened to him…what makes anyone so mean?"

"Life. Some people have it better than others."

"It sounds like you're making excuses for him."

"Not at all. Who knows what happened to Aaron. Maybe he came from an abusive home. Maybe he didn't have a father. Or a mother. Or anyone to love him, but we all have choices to make. We can be bitter or better."

Feeding bitterness had almost totally blinded me to God's goodness and love. "You're right."

He kissed my forehead. "Of course, I am."

"So it really is over. You. Elizabeth…we can go back to the way things were."

"I hope not. In a few days, we may not all be living under the same roof, but I don't think things with the three of us will ever be the same. We've grown closer. Stronger." That familiar hint of mischief flared in his eyes. "Maybe found out things about ourselves and each other we didn't know before."

Like how much I really could care for a man…the right man? "I'll always be grateful for everything you and Elizabeth have done for me, and for your friendship. From the very beginning, the two of you showed me kindness when I was anything but kind."

A huge smile broadened his face. "You weren't unkind. You were skittish."

"I still am. I'm afraid of getting hurt. I'm afraid, when I tell you how I first turned my back on God when Mama died, you'll think less of me. Or you'll run like a scalded dog when I confess I hated my dad growing up. Truth be known, part of me still does. And because of him, my motto regarding men has always been *Not Ever*. Never trust, never let my guard down, and certainly never fall in love…until now."

"Ah, Mamie." He folded me in his arms. "There's nothing you can say that'll change my feelings for you. I do love you, Miss Eisenhower."

Weeks later, Janie, Susie, Travis, Quinn, and I, along with Christopher and Elizabeth, gathered at Susie's for what had become our time for good food, fun games, and great company. Only this week was special. We were celebrating Christopher and Elizabeth's recent engagement.

Quinn lifted his bottle of Dr Pepper toward the adorable couple. "May God bless you two with a long happy marriage."

The sound of glass clanking followed shouts of, "Hear, hear."

Quinn circled his arm around me and breathed in my ear, "And may God grant us double portions."

Joyful tears streamed down my face. It had been ten weeks since Mom's death. Nine of them in Mountain Home. Some would say a stranger and a coin toss decided my fate, but I knew different. God had shown His mercy and given me hope, a new life, and a miracle of miracles, a new kind of love. I had found paradise.

The End

Acknowledgments

To all my family and friends for your continued encouragement, thank you.

A special thanks to my brother, Thomas, for your constant support and advice, which means more to me than you'll ever know.

And to my editor and coach from Brilliant Cut Editing, you are an amazing gift. I've said it many times before, you make my writing shine. Then you designed the perfect cover to house those words and story. Wow!

Kevin Bodhamer with the historic society in Mountain Home, along with his mother—what a wealth of information. I thank you.

My biggest fan and cheerleader, my husband, I can't imagine my life without you. You make life fun!

About the author

Amanda and her husband, both natives of Mississippi, now reside in the beautiful Appalachian mountains of Tennessee.

When Amanda's not writing, she loves trying her hand at gardening and canning. But mostly she enjoys quiet time with her husband, reading, taking care of her goats and chickens, and traveling to those out-of-the-way places full of history, character, and characters.

Chocolate makes everything better, is her motto. Chocolate cream pie is her favorite. But Hershey's syrup on marshmallows always works well in a pinch.

Visit Amanda at www.amandasueking.com.

She'd love to hear from you. A review on the site where you purchased *Not Ever* would be greatly appreciated. And don't forget to check out her first book, *Hidden Scars*.

Amanda Sue King's first book,
Hidden Scars.

For most of her seventeen years, Morgan Selby dreams of a better life. One without beatings and contemptuous words. College Scholarships provide an opportunity. But her parents, who reluctantly allow her to leave, refuse to relinquish their hold. Phone calls, threats, and surprise visits fuel her with paralyzing fear.

When Chuck Mattews, her forbidden love, proposes and wants to marry right away, Morgan's hope fades with memories of her mother's cruel, unfounded accusation, "we know you've had sex", and her dad waving a gun with a promise, "I'll kill him". Besides, in Mississippi, the legal age for marriage is twenty-one. None of this detours Chuck. Not even when Morgan receives word her parents are having her watched. Will she ever be free? More important, how does she ever find the courage to face her parents and ask the question—why?

Available on Amazon in print and Kindle.

www.ingramcontent.com/pod-product-compliance
Lightning Source LLC
Chambersburg PA
CBHW050929120626
46552CB00001B/112